THE ADVENTUROUS FOUR

STRANDED!

THE ADVENTUROUS FOUR

STRANDED!

by
ENID BLYTON

Illustrated by Gavin Rowe

AWARD PUBLICATIONS LIMITED

For further information on Enid Blyton please visit *www.blyton.com*

ISBN 978-1-84135-735-5

This edition published by permission of Chorion Rights Limited

First published 1947 by Newnes as *The Adventurous Four Again*
First published by Award Publications Limited 2003
This edition first published 2009

Published by Award Publications Limited,
The Old Riding School, The Welbeck Estate,
Worksop, Nottinghamshire, S80 3LR

09 1

Printed in the United Kingdom

CONTENTS

CHAPTER ONE

BACK WITH ANDY AGAIN

Three very excited children bumped along a rough country lane in a farmer's ancient estate car. The Scottish driver sat silently in front, listening with a little smile to the happy voices.

"Won't it be great to see Andy again – we haven't seen him for months!" said Tom, a red-haired boy of twelve.

"It was bad luck getting chicken-pox, so we couldn't come up here in the Christmas holidays," said Zoe, and her sister Pippa agreed. They were twins, and very alike. They both had long golden plaits and blue eyes.

Their elder brother, Tom, spoke to the driver. "Jock! Did you hear about our adventures last year?" he asked.

Jock nodded his head and smiled at the memory. The children, with their friend Andy, had indeed had some thrilling adventures. They'd gone out in Andy's father's fishing boat one day and been caught by a storm. They'd been swept miles off their course to a lonely island – and found a secret foreign submarine base in the waters there.

"And poor Andy lost his father's boat," said Zoe.

"But it didn't matter, because Andy was given a much, much better boat!" said Pippa. "And it was called *Andy*. Wasn't he pleased!"

Andy had been more than pleased, because a fishing boat was essential for his father's work, and now they had one of the finest boats on the coast.

The car jolted along, and soon the children came in sight of the sea. The coast was rocky and dangerous, but the sea was a lovely blue.

"The sea! There it is! And look, there are fishing boats out on it!" they all shouted in joy.

"I can see Andy's boat!" cried Tom.

Andy was out there on the restless sea, and soon they would be with him. What fun they would have!

"A whole month by the sea with Andy and his boat!" said Tom. "I can't think of anything better. I don't expect we'll have any adventures this time, but that doesn't matter."

"We had enough last summer to last us for years," said Zoe. "Oh look, there's Mummy!"

Their mother had gone to the little cottage in the Scottish fishing village two days earlier to get everything ready for the children's Easter holidays. Now she was standing at the next corner, waving. The children tumbled out of the car and flung themselves on her.

"Mummy! It's lovely to see you. Is everything all right?"

"Is the cottage ready? Have you seen Andy?"

"I'm hungry. Is there anything nice to eat?" That was Tom, of course. He was always hungry. His mother laughed.

"Welcome back, children! Yes, there's plenty to eat, Tom. And yes, I've seen Andy. He was sorry he couldn't meet you, but there's a good shoal of fish in, and he had to help his father in the boat."

"Does the boat go well?" asked Tom eagerly. "I've often thought of Andy while we were at school, and envied him. There he was, sailing out in all weathers having a wonderful time, while I was writing French exercises and being told off for throwing a rubber at someone."

"Oh Tom, don't tell me your report is a bad one!" said his mother, as they all walked down to the fishing village below. Jock followed, carrying large suitcases as if they were empty boxes!

"When will Andy be back?" asked Zoe. "Has he changed?"

"Of course," said her mother. "He's grown a bit taller and a bit broader, but he's almost fifteen now, you know. You'll see him later this evening, when the fishing boats come back. He promised to come straight up and see you."

"We'll go down to the shore and wait for him," said Tom. "After we've had something to eat, I mean. What is there, Mum?"

"Ham, eggs, three kinds of scone, two kinds of jam, and a fish pie," said his mother. "Will that do?"

"I should think so," said Tom, who felt

as if he could eat the whole lot at once. "Oh, it's good to be back. Think of all the sailing we'll do!"

"Well, don't find any foreign submarines this time," said his mother, as she swung open a gate that led through a tiny garden to the cottage. "I really couldn't bear it if you got lost again."

The children ran up to the wooden door, which had been left open. A fire blazed in the living-room, and the table was piled with food. Tom gave a whoop of delight.

"Wow! Do I have to wash my hands? Can't we begin now?"

"No, wash first," said his mother firmly. "You all look like sweeps. Would you like boiled eggs to begin with, or fish pie?"

"Both!" shouted Tom, as he rushed off to wash.

They all had an enormous meal. "I can see I shall have my work cut out to satisfy your appetites!" said their mother. "No, you needn't clear away and wash up, I've got Mrs MacIntyre coming in to help. Put on your jerseys and shorts and you can go down to meet Andy – I expect the boats will be coming in soon."

They raced down to the shore. Fine, soft sand lay between the rocks that jutted up all over the beach. A stone jetty ran a short distance into the water. To this jetty the fishing boats came with their hauls.

Andy's boat was visible a good way out. But the boats were mostly coming in – the *Seagull*, the *Sally-Ann*, the *Jessie*, the *Andy*, the *Starfish* and the rest. The breeze filled the sails and they billowed out prettily.

Tom ran up and down the jetty with excitement. "I wish I had a boat of my own! Andy, Andy! Arrive first, show us what your boat can do!"

Almost as if Andy had heard, the red-sailed boat surged in front of the others.

"Andy, we're here! Have you made a good catch?" shouted Zoe.

"Ahoy there!" came Andy's voice. "Ahoy!"

Then the beautiful boat came deftly to the stone jetty and Andy leaped off. He and Tom shook hands, both grinning widely. The twins flung themselves on the boy and hugged him, laughing happily.

"Andy, you've grown! Andy, you're browner than ever! Oh, Andy, we're all

back together again, isn't it fantastic?"

"Great," said Andy, as pleased as they were.

Then his father jumped out to tie up the boat. He smiled at the three children, and shook hands with them all. He never had much to say, and the children knew he was strict with Andy, and made him work hard. But they liked him and trusted him.

"You'll help with the fish, Andy," he said, and the boy turned at once to bring in their great catch. The children helped too.

"Can we go sailing with you this evening, Andy?" asked Tom.

"No, not today," said Andy, knowing that his father would not let his boat out again. "Tomorrow perhaps, if we're allowed. Dad may not want the boat tomorrow. We've had such a good catch today."

"Is it nice to see your own name painted on your boat?" said Pippa. "It looks brilliant."

"It's your boat too," said Andy. "I always told you you could share it when you were here. It ought to be called the *Andy-Tom-Zoe-and-Pippa*!"

As the other boats came in, the children

greeted the fishermen. They knew them all and their fine little fishing boats that bobbed gently up and down beside the jetty.

"It's getting dark," said Tom, with a sigh. "We'd better go home. We promised Mum we'd be in before dark, and after our long journey, I do feel tired. All I want to do now is fall into bed and sleep!"

"What, you don't want any supper?" said Zoe. "You *must* be tired, Tom!"

Andy laughed. He was happy to see his friends again. Four whole weeks together! They would have fun.

"See you tomorrow," said Andy.

The children turned away from the shore and went back to the cottage. After a quick supper, they undressed quickly, washed and fell into their beds, half asleep before their heads touched the pillow.

CHAPTER TWO

OFF ON A SAILING TRIP

The next few days were lovely. Andy took them sailing and they went out fishing with the rest of the fleet. He taught them how to let down the nets and how to set lobster-pots in the right places. They took home enough fish and shellfish to keep them in food for a week!

The sun shone. They grew brown. They climbed the rocky cliffs and had a wonderful time. Then Tom grew restless.

"Can't we take the *Andy* and go on a longer trip somewhere?" he said. "Don't you know anywhere exciting you could take us, Andy?"

"Well," said Andy, "I promised your mother I wouldn't take you right out to sea after what happened last year. So it would have to be somewhere along the coast."

"Think of somewhere," begged the twins. "Somewhere that nobody goes to."

"There's the Cliff of Birds," said Andy suddenly.

"The Cliff of Birds," said Zoe. "What a funny name!"

"It's a good name," said Andy. "Thousands of different birds nest there. Gulls, shags, cormorants, puffins. I couldn't tell you how many kinds! They say you can't walk a step at this time of year without treading on a nesting bird. They're really something to see."

The children's eyes shone.

"Let's go!" said Tom. "What a sight it would be! I'll take my camera. We're having a photo competition at my school next term, and I could enter some bird pictures for it."

"Oh yes," said Zoe. "It does sound exciting. Why haven't you ever told us about the Cliff of Birds before, Andy?"

"Well, last time you were here, it was summer," said Andy. "The birds have left their nesting places on the cliffs by then, and are out on the open sea. There's not much to see."

"How far is it?" said Tom. "Can we get there and back in a day?"

"We'll have to," said Pippa. "Mummy won't let us stay a night."

"If we start early in the morning we'll be back before dark," said Andy. "It's a long way, and it's a lonely part of the coast too. We'll have to be careful because there are many hidden rocks, but my father knows a passage between them and I've been with him twice."

"Shall we go tomorrow?" asked Zoe, getting excited.

"No – I'm wanted on the boat with my father," said Andy. "But maybe the day after that."

All the next day the children pored over their bird books. They learned the names of each seabird so they would recognise them when they reached the cliff. Tom put a new roll of film in his camera, while the girls told their mother where they were going.

"It certainly sounds exciting," she said. "I hope Andy knows the way down the coast. It's rather dangerous!"

"Oh, Mum, Andy could sail a boat anywhere!" said Tom, appearing from his bedroom. "He's been twice before, anyway, with his dad. Won't it be exciting to go somewhere that nobody ever goes to?"

The children set their alarm clocks for dawn the next morning, and awoke with a start when it went off. How early it was! Tom slipped into the girls' room.

"The sky's just turning silvery in the east," he said. "Hurry up – we've got to be at the jetty in a few minutes. I bet Andy's already there."

Their mother appeared in her dressing-gown, looking sleepy. "I thought I'd see you off," she said. "Now, promise to be careful. Andy's got life-jackets on board, hasn't he?"

"Oh, Mummy, you know we can all swim like fish!" said Zoe.

"Yes, in calm water," said her mother. "But if you fell overboard in stormy waters you'd find things much more difficult. You've packed some food on board, haven't you?"

"Oh, yes," said Tom, who could always be trusted to look after the food side. "We put everything you gave us on board yesterday evening. It'll last us nicely for a day."

"It would last most families for a week!" said his mother. "Now, are you ready? Take warm jackets with you, because it isn't summer, you know. Tom, where's your anorak?"

Soon they were ready to leave. The children raced down to the jetty, feeling the cool wind on their faces and their bare legs.

Andy was waiting for them. He grinned when he saw their excited faces. "Get on board," he said. "Everything's ready. I'll cast off."

The children tumbled on to the fishing boat, which was roomy, but not too big for them to handle. It even had a small, cosy cabin below.

The boat slid away from the jetty. The breeze filled the sail. Then, quite suddenly it seemed, the sun appeared above the skyline. "The sun's rising," said Zoe, and caught her breath at the sudden beauty of it all. "The world's all new again. Look, the sun seems to be climbing out of the sea!"

Soon they could no longer look at the sun, it was so big and bright.

"Heaps of people have never seen the sun rise," said Zoe. "Hardly any of the girls at my school have. They've missed something! I think there ought to be a law that says everyone must watch a sunrise, and everyone must see a bluebell wood, and a buttercup field, and . . ."

"Look out!" yelled Andy, as the big red sail swung across. Zoe ducked, and forgot what she was saying. Andy was at the tiller, looking browner than ever. His eyes shone as blue as the sea.

"Hey," began Tom, "isn't it about time to . . ."

". . . have something to eat!" they all chanted, knowing what Tom was like.

"I wasn't going to say that," said Tom, indignantly. "I *was* going to say, shouldn't we keep closer to the shore now? We're heading right out to sea."

"Got to," said Andy, keeping a firm hold on the tiller as the boat swept into a strong current. "There are rocks further in. We must keep out here till I see the spot my father told me of, then I'll swing inland."

Andy had a rough chart with him. He passed it to Tom, holding on to it until the boy had it safely because of the rushing wind.

"Look," he said. "Those dots are rocks. Sly rocks they are, just below the surface. They'll scratch a hole in the bottom of a boat in the twinkling of an eye. It'll take us longer to go out to sea, and then turn in, but it's safer. Let me know when you can see three tall pine trees on that cliff, then we can turn. They're marked on the map."

Everyone studied the map with interest. What a long way down the coast the Cliff of

Birds was! No wonder they had to start early.

"What time do you think we'll get there?" asked Pippa.

"We should be there about eleven, with luck," said Andy. "Maybe before. We'll have our lunch then!"

Tom looked alarmed. "What! Wait till then? We'll be starved!"

"Oh, we'll have breakfast first," said Andy. "At seven, or half past. Maybe a few biscuits now would be nice. What do you say?"

Everyone thought it was a very good idea. "Biscuits *and* chocolate!" said Zoe. "They go so well together."

She disappeared down below, and came back again with four rations of biscuits and chocolate. Everyone was soon munching, Andy still at the tiller. He said he was not going to let anyone else steer the boat that day, it was too dangerous!

The sun was much higher in the sky now. It was warmer, though the strong sea breeze was cold. Everyone was glad of their anoraks on top of woollen jerseys.

"Now, here's where we head inland," said

Andy suddenly. "See those three pine trees on the cliff?"

"You've got eyes like a hawk, Andy," said Tom, screwing up his eyes to try and see the trees on the distant coast.

Andy swung the boat round a little. The sail flapped hard. The little boat now ran even more quickly and the children felt a thrill.

"Breakfast time!" said Andy. "We're doing very well, we deserve a really good breakfast!"

"We *do*!" said Tom, and scurried to get the food.

CHAPTER THREE

THE CLIFF OF BIRDS

Breakfast was a feast. There were hard-boiled eggs, scones and butter and a tin of peaches. Zoe heated some milk and made cocoa.

Now that the boat was heading shorewards, the rocky cliffs could be seen clearly.

"Wow, what a desolate coast!" said Tom, as the boat sped along. "And look at those wicked rocks nearer the shore."

"Yes, there are some out here too, so we've got to keep a look-out," said Andy. "The worst are marked on the chart. In about an hour's time we have to slip between an opening in a rocky ridge, and squeeze between two rows of rocks in a kind of channel. We're all right once we get into the channel; it's like a pathway."

At about nine o'clock the children saw a turbulent stretch of water ahead of them. The waves frothed and surged and sent spray blowing high into the air.

"Look!" said Tom, pointing ahead. "There must be rocks there."

"Yes, just about here is the opening I told you about," said Andy. "We've got to slip through it as soon as we come to it. I think it lies beyond that big surge of water."

He cleverly skirted the bubbling, frothing patch, where the waves were torn into shreds on hidden rocks. Then the children gave a shout.

"Here's the entrance, look, a nice calm little bit!"

Andy steered the boat deftly through the rocks at the opening of the passage. The boat careered along, its sail full of wind, and slid into the channel of calm water.

"How far does this channel go, Andy?" asked Pippa.

"It flows to Smugglers' Rock," said Andy, "but we swing towards land before we get there, to the Cliff of Birds."

"Smugglers' Rock! What an exciting name! I wonder why it was given it. Were there smugglers there in the old days?"

"I don't know," said Andy. "I've only seen it from a distance. It's like a small steep island made entirely of rock, but maybe there are caves there that smugglers hid things in. Nobody goes there now, and maybe they never did! Maybe it's just a name."

"It's half past ten," said Tom, after a time. "Are we nearly at the Cliff of Birds?"

"Why, are you getting hungry again?" asked Andy, with a grin.

"Well, I am," said Tom, "but I wasn't thinking of that. I was thinking of the time, and how long we'd have."

"We'll have a couple of hours at the cliffs and no more," said Andy. "But it will be enough. You'll be able to climb up and explore a bit, take some photographs and have lunch. Then we'll have to go back."

"Look, is that Smugglers' Rock over there?" shouted Zoe, pointing westwards. The others turned, and saw a small rocky island rising above the waves a fair distance away. Almost at the same moment Andy swung the boat to the left and headed for the shore.

"Yes, that's Smugglers' Rock," he said. "But I've swung away now, because we're coming to the Cliff of Birds. See the birds bobbing on the water, and flying above it!"

As they sailed nearer, the children shouted in amazement. Birds could be seen everywhere. Gulls called, and the sound of their laughing voices echoed all round them.

"When we round this rocky point, we'll come into a kind of shallow bay," said Andy. "The cliffs behind are the ones I've brought you to see. They're covered with little narrow ledges that seabirds have used to nest on for hundreds of years."

The *Andy* rounded the point, and the children gazed at the towering cliffs, too astonished to speak. There were birds there by the thousand! They lined every ledge, they called from every point. They soared and glided on the currents of air, crying and screeching at the tops of their voices.

The sight of the red-sailed ship startled them. A large flock flew up from the cliffs, and their flight startled hundreds more. The rushing of wings sounded like a mighty wind. Tom gave a cry.

"What's that falling down the cliff? Look, it's like a shower of white drops tumbling down!"

"Eggs!" said Andy. "These seabirds lay their eggs on the bare ledges of rock and they are so careless with them. When they fly off suddenly they often make their precious eggs fall and smash on to the rocks below."

"What a waste," said Pippa. "I wish we hadn't frightened them. But what a sight! I've never, never, in all my life seen or heard so many birds together before!"

"Andy, look, there's a river rushing out at the bottom of the cliff," said Tom, excited. "*Is* it a river? It seems to be coming out of a cave! Right from the depths of the cliff."

"Yes, it's a river," said Andy, bringing in the boat gently. "It must flow right through the cliff. Look, do you see that waterfall splashing halfway down the cliff?"

"It's a very exciting place," said Zoe. "I wish the birds wouldn't make quite so much noise, though. I can hardly hear myself speak!"

"Where are we going to put the boat?" asked Pippa. "There's no jetty, and no sand to drag her on to. What shall we do?"

"I'll guide her into the deep pool under that overhanging cliff," said Andy. "And let down the anchor. We can jump across to the rocks nearby."

"Let's have lunch first," said Zoe.

"Well, just a snack now," said Tom, to everyone's surprise. "I'm longing to explore that cliff. It's incredible, really incredible. We don't want to waste too much time eating. If we had a snack now, we could have a good meal on the way back."

"Right," said Andy. So they hurriedly made some sandwiches of bread and butter and tinned ham. They ate them, had a drink, and then, with the *Andy* lying quietly at anchor, looked to see which rock would be the best to jump to.

"There's a rock just underwater here," said Zoe, peering over the side of the boat. "We'll tread on that, and then we can easily get to that big rock there, and so to the ledge at the bottom of the cliff."

They took off their shoes and strung them round their necks. Then they made their way across the rocks. Not far off, where the river's current met the waves of the sea, the waters boiled and surged.

"I'll find the easiest path up the cliff," said Andy, who was as sure-footed as a goat.

"Follow me carefully. It's steep, but not dangerous to people like us who are used to climbing about. Look out for slippery bits."

The children began their climb. There were plenty of good footholds and handholds, but their parents would certainly not have liked to watch them going slowly upwards, higher and higher, until they looked like specks.

Soon they came to the nesting places, high up above the stormy waves. The frightened, angry birds flew away. There were no real nests and Pippa was upset to see yet more eggs roll into the sea.

"Some of them don't fall off," she called. "They just roll round and round. Look, they're a funny shape; really pointed at one end."

"Eggs shaped like that don't roll away so easily," said Andy. "They are meant to roll round in exactly the same spot."

About halfway up, they came to a narrow ledge that was like a path round the cliff side. The ledge was a popular nesting place, and the children had to be careful not to tread on the eggs. Soon the rocky path widened out into a good resting place, with a shallow cave at the back of it. The children crawled into it and lay there, exhausted from their climb.

"I'll just go out and take a few snaps," said Tom, after a while. But just as he was about to go, he stopped. He heard a noise that sounded very peculiar in that deserted, seabird-haunted place; the sound of somebody whistling! How very strange!

CHAPTER FOUR

A REAL PUZZLE

The whistling sounded loud and clear. The children listened in astonishment. Who could it be? A clamouring of seabirds began again and drowned out the whistling. The children looked at one another.

"Did you hear that?" said Tom, puzzled.

"Let's see who it was," said Andy, and he jumped up. Pippa pulled him back.

"He might be cross if he knew we were here. He might be a bird-watcher or a photographer or something, and if he thought we had disturbed the birds, he'd be angry."

"Well, it's our cliff as much as his," said Andy, shaking his shoulder free from Zoe's hold. The whistling started again, and a scraping sound told the children that the whistler must be coming near.

"He's just above us!" said Zoe, in a startled whisper. "Oh, look!"

Above the cave was a narrow ledge. The whistler had sat himself down on it, for a pair of bare legs suddenly dangled down.

The children didn't like the look of the legs at all. They were covered with thick black hairs, like the fur of an animal, and on the end of them were enormous, dirty feet.

The whistling continued. Then some eggs landed on the rocky ledge in front of the cave. They were flung down deliberately to make a splash as they smashed. The children felt indignant. What kind of person would break birds' eggs on purpose?

No one said a word. There was something about those great legs that made them feel rather afraid. Whoever was up there thought he was alone, and he surely would be the kind of fellow who wouldn't welcome children at all! Whoever could he be?

And how could he have come to the Cliff of Birds? The children had seen no boat in the bay below. They hoped that the man wouldn't spot their boat, either.

"Let's get to the back of the cave," whispered Tom. "In case that fellow comes down a bit lower and sees us."

They wriggled back. They could still see the legs, with their big ugly feet. Then they saw something else. The man was swinging a pair of binoculars.

The whistling stopped. "Twelve o'clock," said a growling voice. The binoculars disappeared, and the children wondered if the man was using them. What was he looking for? Something at sea?

There was a low exclamation. Clearly the man had seen what he wanted. The children strained their eyes, trying to see if any ship was on the horizon, but they couldn't see anything.

After a while the man got up. There was a scrambling noise and a few bits fell from the ledge as the man walked off. The whistling sounded again, but stopped after a little. Then there was silence.

Andy crawled out of the cave and listened cautiously. Nothing. He went out on to the ledge and peered up. He came back to the children.

"Not a thing in sight," he said. "I wonder how he got here?"

"He must have come overland if he hasn't got a boat," said Tom. Andy shook his head.

"No. There's no way overland. Never has been. People always had to come here by boat. The cliff is unclimbable the other side."

"Well, he must have come by boat then!" said Tom.

"Then where has he hidden it?" said Andy. "We would have seen it if it had been there. It's impossible to hide a boat in this shallow bay."

"Where's he gone now?" asked Zoe. "Up the cliff path?"

"He must have," said Andy, "but I

36

always thought the path stopped not far above. Perhaps there's a cave where he's living. I've a good mind to go and see!"

"No, don't," said Zoe. "I didn't like the look of his legs at all. I'm sure he is a huge, ugly, hairy kind of man – like a big gorilla!"

"Don't be stupid!" said Tom. "He may be quite nice. Though I must say I don't think he is, somehow!"

"Well, I'm going to find out where he's gone," said Andy, getting up. "After all, even if he sees me, what does it matter? Anyone can come here and watch the birds."

"I'll come too," said Tom. "I've had enough of resting. You two stay here. We won't be long."

The girls lay back and listened to the sound of the boys climbing up to the ledge above the cave entrance.

"The ledge makes a kind of narrow path here," they heard Tom say. "Come on, he must have gone this way!"

In places the path was nothing but a goat track. There were no goats though, for there was not enough there for even a goat to eat! Very little grew on the rocky cliff, except for a hardy cushion of sea-pinks here and there.

As they rounded a corner they heard a rushing sound. The next moment they saw the waterfall. It was a magnificent sight. The torrent of water flung itself out of the cliff in a slight arch and then fell headlong downwards, gleaming and glittering as it went.

"I wish the girls could see this," said Tom. "Let's go back and get them."

"There's no time," said Andy. "It's odd that we haven't spotted that man yet, isn't it, Tom? There's been no place he could hide in on our way here. Where's he gone?"

"Beyond the waterfall, of course!" said Tom.

"He couldn't go beyond," said Andy. "The water completely bars the way. Who could get through that terrific gush? He'd be swept down the cliff!"

The boys stood beside the waterfall. Tom gazed at the water. He felt puzzled. Certainly it was strange to think that the man whose legs they had seen was nowhere about!

"Do you think he's fallen off?" asked Tom.

Andy shook his head. "No. He must be used to these cliffs, or he wouldn't be on them. He's somewhere around."

"Well, *where*?" demanded Tom, exasperated. "We haven't overtaken him, and you say no one could get across this waterfall without being swept down the cliff with it. And you don't think he's fallen off! Then where is he?"

"I don't know," said Andy, frowning. He looked to see if there was a way above the waterfall, but the cliff was smooth and steep. No one could climb over that way. He bent down and looked under the arch of water as it jerked itself from the cliff.

"No. It would be too dangerous to try and creep under that," he said. "And anyway there doesn't seem to be a ledge the other side. What a puzzle!"

They turned to go back, quite baffled. As they made their way along the ledge the noise of the waterfall seemed to lessen. The boys looked back.

"The torrent isn't so strong – look!" said Tom.

"It probably varies," said Andy. "After heavy rain I expect the waterfall gets enormous. And then in a very dry spell in summer there would hardly be any water coming out at all."

"It's funny, the waterfall has almost stopped now," said Tom, standing and looking at it. "Just a trickle coming out! I wonder why."

"Come on," said Andy, getting impatient. "The girls will be wondering where we are."

They made their way back to the cave, where the girls were anxious to hear what they'd found.

"Not a sign of that man," said Tom, to their great astonishment. "He's simply vanished into thin air! Strange, isn't it?"

"Vanished?" said the twins in surprise. "But where could he have gone?"

"It's getting late, we ought to get back to the boat," said Andy. "Also, I'm hungry – we've only had a snack so far."

They started to go down, but when they had gone just a little way, they heard a surprising sound.

"That whistle again!" said Andy. "Well, the man *is* somewhere about then! Where in the world is he hiding?"

CHAPTER FIVE

A Good Trip Back

Andy stopped and looked around, but he could see nothing. "We don't have time to go back and have another look," he said. "But, really, where could the man have been, Tom?"

"Beats me," said Tom. "But never mind! I want my lunch much more than I want to know where that man hid!"

So down they went. It was much easier to go down than up. After a while they all stood safely on the rock at the bottom of the cliff. They clambered aboard their boat, and went down into the cabin to get some food. Cold ham. Hard-boiled eggs. Rolls. And a big tin of sliced peaches. What a lovely meal!

"There's chocolate if anyone's still hungry," said Zoe. "Mummy has put in dozens of bars of fruit and nut!"

"Have we time to eat our lunch here, or

41

must we set sail straight away?" asked Tom.

Andy looked at the sun. "It's a good way past noon," he said. "I think we'd better leave now, and eat our lunch as we go. The wind has shifted, so it won't help us going back."

The boys rowed until they reached the open sea. Soon they were speeding along again. The four children sat on deck in the sunshine and ploughed their way hungrily through the food.

"We'll be back just before dark," said Andy. "Look, here's where the channel goes off to Smugglers' Rock. See?"

The children looked at the water that lay in the channel between the two ridges of rock, and screwed up their eyes to have another look at the eerie, steep rocky island called Smugglers' Rock. Yes, there it was in the distance, a desolate, lonely rock, where nobody ever went.

"Shall we go there one day, Andy?" asked Tom. "We could hunt for the caves the smugglers used."

"All right," said Andy. "If you like. It's a nice sailing trip."

The children enjoyed being in the *Andy*. They loved the flapping of her sail and the creaking noise she made. They liked the lapping of the water against her hull, and the wake that spread behind them like a feathery tail.

"I think all children ought to have a boat of their own," said Tom. "I wish I had a boat, and a horse and a dog, and . . ."

He stopped suddenly, and looked incredibly upset.

"What's the matter?" said Zoe.

"Guess what I've done?" said Tom. "I've left my camera behind! My best camera, the one Dad gave me at Christmas. I promised to be careful with it. But now I've gone and left it on the Cliff of Birds!"

"Idiot!" said Pippa. "You're so careless. Mummy will be furious."

"Well, one of you might have noticed I'd left it behind," said Tom crossly. "Andy, can we turn back?"

"Don't be stupid," said Andy. "We haven't got time, you know that. I'm not steering this boat through these dangerous waters in the dark."

"I didn't take any snaps, and now I've lost my camera," lamented Tom. "It's such a beauty too. I must have left it at the back of that cave. Golly, I hope the whistling man doesn't find it!"

Tom looked so distraught that Andy was sorry for him. "Cheer up," he said. "We'll go back for it later this week. If my father can spare the boat, we'll sail to the Cliff of Birds again, and maybe visit Smugglers' Rock!"

Everyone cheered up. That would be brilliant! They would start off even earlier, or perhaps their mother would let them spend the night on board the boat. They began to talk about it, their eyes shining.

"Don't be too hopeful," said Andy, steering the boat deftly between the two dangerous ridges of rock. "You know what happened last time your mother gave you permission to spend a night or two on a sailing trip!"

"Well, nothing like that could happen here," said Tom, looking at the desolate, lonely coast they were passing. "Why, there isn't a ship or a plane to be seen."

"Then I wonder what that man was looking for with his binoculars," said Zoe.

They began to talk again about how he could have disappeared.

"I tell you, there wasn't a hole big enough to hide even a rabbit," said Tom. "He just vanished into thin air!"

"Well, he came back again from thin air all right!" said Pippa, with a laugh.

Suddenly Zoe sat upright on the deck. "I know!" she said. "I know where he went! I bet he waited until the waterfall grew smaller and then he shot into the opening the water pours from, and made his way into the cliff from there!" she said triumphantly.

"What, do you mean you think the man

got into the cliff through the waterfall opening?" said Tom as last. "What an idea! He'd never hide there. He'd be wet through."

"Well, where did he hide, then?" said Zoe. "You can't think of anywhere better. I reckon there's a way into the heart of the cliff just there. I'm sure there is!"

Zoe was very pleased with her idea. She went on talking about it, and gradually she got the others excited. "Zoe may be right," said Andy, his eyes fixed on the waters ahead of him. "It might be possible to get in at the waterfall hole, once the water has lessened."

"Let's go and look when we go back for Tom's camera!" said Pippa. "We must! I can't bear an unsolved mystery!"

"I'd like to find out that man's hiding place and who he is," said Zoe. "But I don't want to have anything to do with him at all!"

"We'll keep out of his way all right," said Andy. "Here, Tom, would you like to take the tiller for a little while?"

Tom took the tiller eagerly. The girls lay down on the rugs on the deck, enjoying the warm sunshine. The boat careered on joyfully.

"She's a happy boat," said Pippa drowsily. "She likes us coming out in her. Phew, I do feel sleepy. Wake me up at teatime!"

They had tea at five o'clock, when the sun was sliding down in the west. As it went behind the clouds and an evening chill crept over the sea, everyone put on an extra jumper and then an anorak.

"We'll be home before it's dark," said Tom. "We've had a lovely day. It was fun climbing up that cliff, and seeing all those birds."

"And it will be fun to go back and see if there really is a hiding place behind that waterfall," said Zoe. "And I'm looking forward to going to Smugglers' Rock. When can we go?"

"I think the weather's changing," said Andy, gazing at the sky. "It looks like rain is setting in. We must choose a fine day to go off again. It would be a really uncomfortable trip in bad weather."

They got in just as heavy drops of rain began to fall. Their mother was relieved to see them, but she was upset when she heard that Tom had left his camera behind.

"You'll have to go and get it," she said. "It's much too good to leave lying about. How careless you are, Tom! And it's not the first time this has happened. It's no good giving you anything nice!"

"I'm terribly sorry, Mum," said Tom. "I promise that we'll go and get it the first fine day we have."

CHAPTER SIX

SAILING AWAY AGAIN

As Andy had foretold, the next few days it rained. But fishing was good, and the children, in macs, boots and waterproof hats, had a lovely time helping out. Andy worked hard. The hauls were excellent and his father was pleased.

"Maybe he'll give me two or three days off," said Andy. "And when the fine weather returns, we can take the *Andy* and go off again."

One night Andy's father came over and the children's mother gave him a delicious supper. The children chattered away like magpies.

"They must make your head ache!" their mother said to Andy's father.

"Och, their chatter is no more than the calling of the gulls!" said the fisherman, with a chuckle.

"But we're much more useful than the

gulls!" said Pippa. "You said we helped you a lot this week!"

"So you have," he agreed. "Andy's taught you a bonny lot of things! You're right good children. You don't mess about and get into mischief like most little scallywags."

This was a long and handsome speech from Andy's father. The children were delighted. Pippa made the most of his good temper.

"Will you be able to let Andy off for a day or two soon?" she asked. "We really want to go out in the *Andy* again by ourselves."

"Well," Andy's father replied, with a smile, "how about the day after tomorrow for a couple of days?"

"Great! That means we can go to Smugglers' Rock!" said Tom.

"Where's that?" asked his mother quickly.

"Oh, it's a place we saw when we went to the Cliff of Birds," said Tom airily. "Mum, as Andy will have two days off, could we spend the whole time on the boat? I'd like time to take some proper pictures at the Cliff of Birds, if I can find my camera again, and we also want to sail to Smugglers' Rock. It looks exciting."

"Not a night out! You know I don't like . . ." began his mother.

"But Andy will look after us, won't he?" said Tom, turning to Andy's father. "Andy's often out all night with you, isn't he?"

"Oh, Andy's used to being on the boat for nights on end!" said the fisherman, in a very good mood after his huge supper. "You'll not come to any harm with Andy there. You can trust my boy, ma'am."

"Oh, I know I can," said the children's mother. "It's only that, well, after last year I don't want them to go out on their own again."

"Why, ma'am, you don't suppose two adventures like that could happen, do you?" said Andy's father. "You let them go, they'll be all right with Andy. He can anchor the boat somewhere quiet, and they can sleep on her in comfort if they take plenty of rugs."

It all seemed to be settled. The children felt very grateful to Andy's father for making things so easy. He seemed to have conquered their mother's fears completely!

The next evening Andy came up to the cottage. "Weather's changing," he said. "See that sky? We'll set off tomorrow. Get what food you can and I'll bring some too. Knowing Tom's appetite I reckon we'd better get a good stash!"

Their mother always told the children to take as many tins as they wanted. They took her at her word and soon the *Andy* was well stocked with all kinds of things, from sardines to tins of pineapple. Andy stared in surprise at the store in the cabin cupboards.

"We won't want all that!" he said. "Well, never mind, we won't bother taking it back now. Got some rugs? We need plenty to sleep on."

Soon there were piles of rugs on board the *Andy* too, and some old cushions from the cottage. It was almost dark before the children had finished packing. They felt as if they were going on a long, long trip. A night away made all the difference!

They set off at eight o'clock in the morning, and their mother came down to the jetty to wave goodbye. Andy took the tiller, and the little boat glided away. Tiny white-topped waves curled against her smooth sides, and she bobbed a little.

"She's happy again!" said Zoe. "And so are we! Goodbye, Mummy! See you tomorrow evening!"

Soon the boat rounded the corner of the rocky bay and went out of sight. The children settled down to enjoy the trip. The wind was strong and the *Andy* galloped along. Pippa, who had lain awake with excitement the night before, fell asleep. Spray splashed over her but she didn't stir. The others chatted, and Zoe once more talked about the hiding place which she felt must be behind the waterfall.

"What I want to know," said Tom, "is where I left my camera. I'm pretty certain I put it down in that cave. I hope it's still there."

Now they were running along the channel and could see Smugglers' Rock in the distance. But they would not go there today, they would go tomorrow!

They turned into the bay they had anchored in before, and at once they heard the terrific clamour of the nesting birds. "Careless birds!" said Zoe. "What do they do when they fly back and see that their eggs are gone?"

"Just lay some more, I suppose," said Tom. "Pippa, wake up! We're here!"

The place seemed as deserted as before. But perhaps the whistling man was hiding somewhere? Or maybe he had gone.

"Let's take some food and have a picnic at that place we rested in before," said Andy. "It has a marvellous view right over the sea. If we find your camera, Tom, you can take some photographs."

Everyone thought this was a good idea, and put what food they wanted into backpacks.

"Ready, everyone?" asked Andy.

They began their steep climb up, following the cat-like Andy who seemed to know all the best handholds and footholds. The hot sun made the climb tiring and they were glad when they reached the resting place. Zoe threw herself down, exhausted. Tom gave a cry of joy and picked up his camera, which was lying at the back of the cave.

"Look! It's here! What a bit of luck. I am pleased."

They had a leisurely meal on the wide ledge, marvelling at the great expanse of slowly-moving blue sea below them.

"I'm glad we haven't got those horrid hairy legs to look at this time!" said Pippa, lying down flat. "Ooh, I'm sleepy again!"

"Well, don't go to sleep, because we want to go and have a look at that waterfall rushing out of the cliff," said Zoe, prodding her.

"Yes, come on," said Andy, getting up. "And be careful along this next path, because it's incredibly narrow in places."

They all went along the ledge to the waterfall. But the torrent of water was not nearly so powerful as before. It was a mere trickle.

"Funny!" said Andy. "I should have thought that with all the rain we've had the waterfall would be pretty big. Come along. We don't need to be afraid of being thrown off the cliff by *that* bit of water! It's no more than a gushing spring!"

They approached the waterfall. Beyond it the cliff ledge came to a sudden end. There was no way around the other side. The water ran out of a hole in the cliff, and fell headlong down. Andy made his way there cautiously and looked into the opening.

He gave a shout, "Anyone could get in here now! Anyone! I bet that's where the man went. He waited till the torrent lessened, then hopped up. That was his hiding place."

"But what's he hiding for?" said Zoe, puzzled. "There's nothing and no one to hide from!"

"Can we get in?" asked Tom excitedly. "Yes, I bet we can."

"No, don't," said Andy. "Suppose the water came out again in a sudden great rush? You'd be sent right off the cliff!"

Tom looked sulky. "All right," he said, and turned back. "Well, the puzzle's solved. That's where the man went. But if you're not going to let us explore any further, we won't know anything else. You're such a wet blanket!"

"Can't help it," said Andy, giving him a little shove. "I'm in charge. Go and take some pictures of birds while the sun is bright!"

Tom didn't argue. But he made up his mind that as soon as the others were not looking, he'd go back to the waterfall and find out more. He'd show Andy he would have his own way!

CHAPTER SEVEN

Tom Knows Best!

"I'd like to explore the rocks at the bottom of the cliff," said Zoe, as they turned back from the waterfall. "I'd like to go to where that underground river comes rushing out. It looks exciting down there."

"Yes, let's do that," said Pippa. "It will be nice to get out of the wind. It's rather cold up here today."

"Right. Let's go down then," said Andy. "Coming, Tom?"

But Tom had other ideas. He called back. "No, not just now. I'm going to try and get some bird pictures. I'll join you later."

"Well, don't be too long!" called back Pippa, beginning to go down the cliff. "And for goodness sake, don't forget your camera this time!"

Tom sat down and looked at the seabirds soaring and gliding in the current of air that blew straight up the cliff. They were magnificent. "I'd better take a few pictures before I try any exploring," he thought. So he crept round the ledge and waited till the seabirds had come back to their eggs, and were sitting on them.

He took a few snapshots that he thought should be very good. Then he put his camera down at the back of the cave again, and made his way round to the waterfall.

His heart beat fast. He knew that Andy would be cross if he found out. "But after all, I'm nearly thirteen, and quite able to look after myself!" thought Tom. "I'm surprised Andy hadn't the guts to go into that waterfall hole himself!"

He came to the waterfall. It was still not much more than a gushing spring and there didn't seem any great danger of a great torrent of water pouring out. Tom peered in cautiously. The water flowed out of a rocky bed and had made a channel for itself. Above, as far as he could see, was a ledge. Anyone getting up there should be quite dry.

He felt in his pocket. Yes, he had his torch. It was wrapped in a few layers of oilskin to protect it from getting wet. He climbed into the rocky hole. It was narrow and he got wet as he went in, but he didn't mind. He dragged himself through the water and up on to the ledge.

Now he was safe from the water, unless of course the torrent suddenly grew bigger and swept out of the hole, filling the opening completely. Tom shivered at the thought. That would not be pleasant! He had better get further inside, then he would feel safer!

He switched on his torch, and looked up the dark tunnel.

"I'll see if I can find that man's hiding place!" thought the boy, feeling excited. "I might find something that would tell me who he is. It seems so funny for someone to be living in this desolate place. Perhaps he's in hiding!"

Tom began to wriggle along the narrow ledge. The roof of the strange little tunnel was low, and it wasn't very comfortable. He put his torch in his teeth so that he had both hands to grasp the rock with and pull himself along. The ledge ran for a few metres, and then dipped a little, so that water ran over it! Bother! Couldn't he get any further along the tunnel?

Tom took the torch out of his mouth and flashed it beyond him. Not far in front he saw the narrow tunnel open out. Into a cave perhaps? He really must go and see, even if it meant a wetting!

This time he had to wriggle through the water on the ledge, and he got his front very wet indeed. But he didn't even feel the icy cold in his excitement. Soon he found that, quite suddenly, the narrow tunnel stopped, and beyond there was an enormous cave! How extraordinary!

The cave had a high roof, an uneven floor, and gleaming walls. The stream that flowed through the tunnel and became the waterfall passed in a channel across its floor; it came from what looked like an entrance to a small cave at the back, but Tom didn't want to go any deeper into the darkness!

Tom flashed his torch around. This would make a brilliant hiding place! It must be where that man had gone. But there was no sign of anyone. It was silent there in the heart of the towering cliff. No sound of calling seabirds came in through the long, narrow entrance. No rush of wind disturbed the still air. It was like being in a curious dream.

"I wish the others were here to share this with me," thought Tom. "I'll go and get them! But first I'll just see if I can find a trace of that whistling man, a cigarette end perhaps, or a match."

He looked around again. Then, out of the corner of his eye, he spotted something gleaming on the floor. Tom wondered what it was and went to pick it up. It was a small pearl button from a man's shirt! But it was red, not white.

Tom looked at it eagerly. This was a sure sign that somebody had come into the cave. But they obviously didn't live there, for there was no sign of a bed or any food stores. Whoever came here must have gone further into the cliff. Perhaps the whole cliff was honeycombed with caves and tunnels! Tom remembered the underground river that flowed out so turbulently at the foot. That must come down winding channels of its own from somewhere!

"I think I'll go back to the others," said Tom to himself. "It's a bit frightening being here in this cliff all by myself. If I stay around, I might get caught by the whistling man and if I go further in I might get lost. I'll go back."

He flashed his torch round the cave once more, and suddenly noticed that the stream had risen higher!

"Look at that!" said Tom in surprise, and he stood watching the water. "Why has it risen like that? It's flooding the floor of this cave!"

So it was. The water rose higher and swept over the floor. It began to make a noise. Tom felt alarmed.

"Oh, no! I know what's happening! The torrent of water further in must have increased and now it's pushing its way out here and will make the waterfall enormous again! If I don't go now I'll be swept down the cliff with the torrent!"

This was not a pleasant thought. Tom ran back to the narrow tunnel. But already the little tunnel was filling with water! The rocky ledge he had wriggled along could hardly be seen, for the water had risen high above it. In a few minutes the opening would be blocked!

"I can't go along it now," thought Tom. "I just daren't."

The water had risen up to Tom's knees. He felt frightened. Perhaps he should go to the inner cave that he had seen? It wasn't safe in this cave now! Who knows how high the water would rise, and there was no place he could climb up to until the water went down again.

"I wish I hadn't explored in here," he thought in dismay. "Now I may be kept a prisoner for hours. What an idiot I am!"

He made his way to the further side of the cave. Water came through a fairly high tunnel from the inner cave and Tom stepped into it. It came to his waist already. He would have to wade along until he came to the inner cave.

Water flooded over the floor of that cave too, but to Tom's surprise and delight, he saw rough steps cut in the wall at the back of the cave. He flashed his torch there. Yes, those steps led to an opening in the cave roof. Up there he would be quite safe from the rising water. Good!

"I wonder if those steps lead into another cave," thought the boy. "This is all very weird. Who would have guessed there were these caves leading one out of the other like this!"

He went up the steps. There was a hole in the roof, and iron footholds had been driven into the rock to help in the climb. Tom put his torch between his teeth again, and hauled himself up. He came out into a dark tunnel that twisted in front of him.

"Well, I suppose I'd better go along," thought Tom, trying to sound much braver than he felt. "It must lead somewhere!"

CHAPTER EIGHT

THE HIDDEN CAVE

Tom went down the winding passage. It smelled horrible. He hoped his torch wouldn't suddenly run out. It would be dreadful to wander about in the dark all by himself!

The tunnel twisted downwards. It was narrow most of the time, and sometimes the roof went low so that Tom had to bend his head down or he would have bumped it. Sometimes the roof became so high that Tom's torch showed him nothing but darkness.

"I'd be enjoying this more if the others were here!" thought Tom, still trying to feel brave. "I really hope this tunnel leads somewhere! I almost wish I could meet the whistling man."

But he met nobody. The tunnel went on and on, always downwards. And then, stealing up it came a familiar smell!

"Tobacco smoke!" he thought. "There must be somebody nearby, smoking a cigarette or pipe. I'd better be careful."

He trod quietly, shielding the light of his torch. Then suddenly he saw a light in the distance! He crept nearer. He could hear voices now, men's voices. One of them was the growly voice of the man with the hairy legs. The boy's heart began to thump. He was glad that people were near, but somehow he felt that they wouldn't welcome him at all!

He tiptoed to the end of the tunnel, and peeped into the cave. He saw two men. One was plainly the hairy-legged man, for his legs were bare, and Tom could see his enormous feet. He was not a giant as the children had imagined, but a curious-looking fellow, with a stumpy body, hairy arms, a big head with hardly any neck, and a flaming-red beard. The other man looked like an ordinary fisherman.

The men sat on boxes, talking. Tom couldn't hear what they were saying. He stared round the cave, astonished, for its sides were piled with wooden boxes and crates. This was clearly a storehouse of some kind. But why? And where did all the boxes come from?

There was a rough mattress in one corner of the cave. One or both men slept there, then. What a curious place to live! Tom was puzzled. But he did feel sure that these men would not welcome his presence there! Whatever they were doing was something they wanted to be kept hidden.

"I daren't ask them for help," thought the boy desperately. "That man with the hairy legs looks as if he'd think as little of hurling me down the cliff as of dropping and smashing those birds' eggs!"

Tom tried to hear what they were saying, but he couldn't make out a word. Perhaps they were talking in some foreign language. Then one of the men looked at his watch. He got up and jerked his head at the other. They went to what appeared to be a hole in the ground, and seemed to drop right down. Anyway, they completely disappeared!

Tom waited a few moments and then cautiously went over and looked down the hole. There was nothing to be seen. The men had gone. Tom didn't feel tempted to follow them. For one thing he couldn't see any steps or footholds to get down the hole! He looked round the cave. He could hardly see its walls, they were stacked so high with boxes. What could be inside them?

The men had left a lantern alight on a box in the middle of the cave. Did that mean they were coming back soon? Tom did not want to be there when they returned. But where could he go? As he stood there thinking, he heard a muffled sound. It seemed to come from somewhere to the left of the big cave.

"It sounds like rushing water," thought Tom. "Whatever can it be?"

Tom went over to a big stack of boxes on the left of the cave. On the wall behind them there was a hole, almost round, about as high as Tom's waist. The rushing noise came from there. Tom poked his head through the hole. He switched on his torch and saw a strange sight. It was an underground river!

"That must be the river that comes out at the foot of the cliff," thought Tom. "If I could follow it, I'd soon be out of here!"

Tom stood and gazed at the swiftly flowing river by the light of his torch. He wondered how far it was from the foot of the cliff. After all, the tunnel he had followed had come down and down and down. Maybe he was almost level with the base of the cliff.

Tom went back into the cave and looked round for another torch. He felt sure his own one wouldn't last much longer and he didn't want to face another long journey without being sure he had plenty of light! Before he could see anything that resembled a torch, he heard the sound of someone scrambling up the hole in the cave floor. Before Tom's startled eyes, the big, bearded face of the man with the hairy legs popped out of the hole! Tom stared at him, petrified. And he stared back at Tom, unable to believe his eyes. A boy! A boy in his cave! Was he dreaming?

Tom swallowed hard, and tried to speak. The bearded face opened its eyes wide, and then the mouth opened too, and a bellow came out.

"What are you doing here?"

Tom couldn't move. His feet seemed to be growing into the ground. He watched the stumpy, short-necked man heave

himself out of the hole and come towards
him. Frightened, he backed away, straight
into the box on which the lamp was set.
The lamp toppled over, flared up, and then
went out. The cave was instantly in
darkness.

The bearded man began to mutter something and to feel about for another light. Tom knew that this was his only chance of escape. He ran softly behind the pile of boxes and was through the hole in the wall in a second.

He had hoped there would be a ledge or a rock of some kind he could hold on to. But there was nothing; only the cold, rushing river!

Tom landed in the water with a splash. Its coldness made him catch his breath. He let himself be carried along as the strong current bore him away rapidly.

"Why did I disobey Andy?" thought Tom dolefully. "I'll never get out of this mess, never! Ooh, how cold the water is!"

The river apparently ran in a deep channel of rock. Tom could not see if they were passing through caves, nor could he see if there were any banks of rock or sand to the river. He just had to go with it, trying to keep his balance. He grew tired and cold. And then, just as he felt he really could not go on any longer, he saw a bright light in front of him, a big, wide, dazzling patch of light that filled him with joy.

"Sunshine!" said Tom. "That's sunshine! I must be near the place where the river rushes out of the cliff!"

He suddenly felt so weak with relief that he lost his balance, and the current took him and rolled him over. He gasped and spluttered trying as best he could to hold his face and shoulders out of the water. As he arrived at the point where the sea and river met, a big wave ran up and caught him.

Luckily, he was thrown sideways onto a rock, and managed to pull himself up out of reach of the water. He couldn't move. He just lay on his back, shivering and trembling, and gasping for breath.

CHAPTER NINE

WHEREVER IS TOM?

Meanwhile, what were Andy, Zoe and Pippa doing? They had been having quite a good time, though not so exciting as Tom.

They climbed steadily down the cliff, to the alarm of all the seabirds they passed. Once more dozens of eggs rolled into the sea as the birds flew off. After some time they came to the foot of the cliff. There were some glorious rock pools there, full of fine sea anemones. The children explored the pools, and disturbed some enormous crabs.

"Look out!" said Andy. "A nip from a big fellow like that won't be very pleasant!"

The wind was not as strong at the foot of the cliff as it was on top, and the sun felt hot. Pippa glanced up.

"I bet Tom's feeling hungry again!" she said. "I'm hungry too, but we'd better wait till Tom comes down before we eat."

"It shouldn't take him long to take a few snapshots," said Andy. "I'm surprised he isn't here by now!"

"Let's go and sit near that river and wait for Tom," said Pippa.

"It would be a great place for a picnic," said Zoe. "I really do feel very hungry. We can give Tom a call when we see him."

They went to where they had anchored the boat. They rummaged about in the cabin for food, finding it hard to choose what to take.

"Sardines, bread and butter, tinned ham, hard-boiled eggs; and tinned plums," said Zoe.

"No, tinned pears," said Pippa. "Those are best. And where's the lemonade?"

They took everything to a high rock overlooking the spot where the river and sea met. They set out the meal, and then looked to see if there was any sign of Tom coming down the cliff. But there wasn't.

"What can he be doing?" said Zoe impatiently. "He's been ages!"

"Well, we'll wait five minutes more, and then begin without him," said Pippa.

They waited, but still there was no Tom.

Andy looked a little worried, but he said nothing. They opened the sardines, spread the butter on their bread, and began a delicious meal. By the end of it there was not much left. And still no Tom!

"Andy, you don't think Tom's in any difficulty, do you?" said Zoe suddenly. "It's so unlike him not to turn up long before a meal."

"Well, I've been thinking that myself," said Andy. "I'd better go up the cliff again and fetch him down."

"What a nuisance he is!" said Pippa.

"Not to worry," said Andy. "You two stay here. It's nice and sunny, and the wind shouldn't be a problem. I'll be as quick as I can."

Off he went. Soon the girls could see him, small and far off, up the cliff side.

"I bet he gives Tom a piece of his mind!" said Zoe, lying on her back, enjoying the feel of the sun-warmed rock.

Andy climbed steadily and at last came to the resting place. There was no one there, but what was this at the back of the cave? Tom's camera! If he was not photographing birds, what was he doing?

And *where* was he? Andy began to feel frightened. He left the camera where it was, and went on to the waterfall. It was now no longer a trickle, but was pouring out in a great cataract! Could Tom have been foolish enough to try and get into the cliff through the waterfall hole? Surely, surely not!

"I told him not to," said Andy, but he couldn't help feeling that Tom would have disobeyed him if he had wanted to badly enough. Andy stood looking at the waterfall for some time, knowing there was nothing to do if Tom really had gone inside. Then, thinking that he should not leave the girls any longer, he started to go back.

As he moved away from the waterfall its noise grew less. Andy turned round and saw that once again it was no more than a gushing spring. He turned to go on and then stopped, his eyes almost falling out! An enormous hairy leg came out of the waterfall! Then another! Andy knew they were the same legs they had seen before. Filled with fear, he climbed hurriedly round the edge of the cliff so as to be out of sight when the man emerged from the hole.

He climbed down steadily, passing the

place where Tom's camera was without stopping. He was just below it, when he heard the growling voice not far away. Then something hurtled past him, something with a long brown strap, and crashed on the rocks below.

Andy climbed down the rest of the cliff as fast as he could. He found the girls sitting on their rock, looking pale and frightened.

"Couldn't find Tom," said Andy. "I think the silly idiot's got inside the waterfall hole. You were right, Zoe, when you said that hairy-legged man hid there. He came out when I was quite near!"

"Andy, look!" said Pippa in a low, scared voice, and pointed to something on a rock not very far away. "It's Tom's camera!"

Pippa burst into tears. The suddenness of the camera falling so near had given her a shock. And now Andy had come back without Tom.

"Andy, what are we to do about Tom?" asked Zoe. "Surely he wouldn't have gone exploring all by himself?"

"Tom can be very foolish at times," said Andy. "I'm afraid he may have been caught by that man. There's something strange going on, which I don't want to be mixed up in. I want to go back home and get Dad."

"But, Andy, we can't go without Tom!" said Pippa. "We can't leave him here all alone."

But Andy stood up. "Collect the things and come back to the boat," he ordered. "We must go."

"No," said Pippa. "I'm not going. I'm not going to desert Tom, even if you are!"

"We're not deserting him," said Andy. "We're going to get help. Come along and don't argue with your skipper."

Zoe began to gather up the things, but Pippa remained obstinate. Andy gave her a rough shake. "Do as you're told! Can't you see I'm worried stiff? It's Tom's disobedience that has led to this. I'm not going to have any more trouble! You'll come along with Zoe and me!"

As they gathered up the last of the tea things, Zoe glanced down at the underground river. Then her eyes widened and her mouth opened to give a cry. But none came. She reached out her arm and pointed.

The others looked. Rolling over and over on the river, swept from side to side like a log, came a strange dark object.

"Andy! It's Tom. Poor, poor Tom!" said Zoe, in a choking voice. "The river's got him."

Andy looked at the tumbling body. He saw it swept to one side, on to the rocks

where river and sea met. Then he saw the tired arms heave up the exhausted body to a place of safety.

"He's all right!" yelled Andy, almost startling the girls out of their skins. "He's all right!"

All three rushed to where Tom lay, slipping and sliding as they went. He looked up at them and grinned feebly.

"Hello!" he said. "Nice to see you all again! I'm sorry to say that we've plunged into the middle of a most exciting adventure! Wait till I've told you everything. Anybody got anything to eat? I'm starving!"

CHAPTER TEN

WHAT HAPPENED ON THE WAY BACK

Andy, Zoe and Pippa were so relieved to see Tom alive and hungry that for a moment they could only stare at him. Then Zoe rushed to get something for him to eat. Andy called after her. "Bring a couple of rugs. He's wet through and shivering."

Soon Tom was sitting in a sheltered corner with a couple of warm rugs tucked round him, munching bread and corned beef, his wet clothes drying in the wind.

"Now, tell us everything!" said Zoe. Tom glanced at Andy, and looked rather embarrassed. He didn't like to own up to his disobedience, which had nearly ended in disaster.

Andy saw the look. "I suppose you got in through the waterfall opening?" he said, not unkindly, but sternly. Tom went red and nodded.

"Yes, I did," he said. "I'm sorry, Andy."

"I'm very glad you're safe," said Andy. "But listen to me, Tom, any more disobedience and you don't come out in my boat again. I'm in charge, and if you can't be loyal to your skipper, you're no use."

"I know, Andy," said Tom humbly. "I've learned my lesson. But wait till you hear!"

"Do tell us!" begged Zoe. "Don't scold him any more, Andy. Let him tell us his story."

So Tom related his adventure, while the others sat listening intently, holding their breath so as not to miss a word!

"Wow!" said Andy. "This is amazing. You were lucky to escape, Tom. But you must have had a shock when you fell into that river."

"I did," said Tom. "But wasn't it lucky that it took me out here?"

"I really can't imagine what those men are up to," said Andy. "Can they be smugglers? But what are they doing inside this cliff? There's no road overland to take smuggled goods. It's a real puzzle."

Tom was feeling much better now. In fact, he was feeling quite a hero! True, he had disobeyed Andy, but things had come out all right, and he had made some exciting discoveries. He began to look a little cocky, but Andy soon put a stop to that.

"I think we should get back home as soon as we can," he said. "Tom will get a chill after falling into the icy river. It's a pity to bring our trip to a sudden end, but I don't want him catching pneumonia!"

Tom's face fell. "I'm perfectly all right, Andy, you know I am."

"Anyway, isn't it too late to start back?" asked Zoe, looking at the sun, which was now well down in the west.

Andy looked at it too and made some calculations. "The wind's in our favour, and we ought to go. Those men may follow us and look out for our boat."

"Bother!" said Tom. "Why did I go and spoil our trip? And we haven't been to Smugglers' Rock either!"

But Andy had made up his mind. "Come on," he said, getting up. "We'd better go."

They went back to the *Andy* with sad faces and set sail. What a sudden end to what had promised to be a really exciting trip! Nobody said anything. They were all

85

disappointed. It was frustrating to leave an unsolved mystery behind. They would have loved to find out why those men were in the cave, what they were doing there, and who they were!

Suddenly Tom gave a yell and pointed ahead, "What's that over there, by those tall rocks?"

Andy's sharp eyes made out what it was at once; a motor-boat! It was lying still, not moving. Could it be waiting for them? When they got nearer, they heard her motor

being started up, and the boat swung out into the centre of the channel down which the *Andy* was flying.

The channel between the two ridges of rock was too narrow for them to get past safely. Andy saw that he would go on the rocks if he tried to swing past! They came up to the motor-boat. A tall, foreign-looking man leaned over the side.

"Who are you? What are you doing here?" he shouted.

"That's none of your business!" shouted back Andy. "Get out of our way!"

"Anchor your boat and come on board," ordered the man.

"Who are you?" bellowed back Andy angrily. "Clear out of our way! We're children out on a sailing trip."

"Andy! Turn back! Let's go back to the Cliff of Birds," begged Zoe. Andy looked scornful, then he glanced at the sky, which was now dark and overcast. In a short time it would be almost dark.

The man, joined by another man, began to yell at Andy again to come on board. Then suddenly a great wave surged up, and took hold of the motor-boat, swinging her round violently. She must have struck a rock just below the surface, for there was a grinding noise and the motor-boat shivered from top to bottom. The men disappeared at once to see what the damage was.

"Now's our chance!" said Andy. "We'll turn and go back, not to the Cliff of Birds, which is where they expect, but to Smugglers' Rock!"

Andy did not think that the motor-boat would dare to come after them in the gathering dark. As soon as he could, he pulled down the sail and took the oars with Tom.

"Look out for the place where the channel forks," he said. "It's a good long row, but never mind!"

Fortunately the current helped them, and it was not as hard as Andy had expected. They slid along the channel, which became wider and approached the tall, steep rock. They could not see it clearly, for it was full of shadows. They took the boat into a small cove. Andy thought they had better drop anchor there and hope for the best. Perhaps they could escape out to sea next day.

"Are we going on to the little island?" asked Zoe.

"No," said Andy. "We shouldn't be able to find our way properly, with the moon slipping in and out of clouds like this. We'll sleep on the boat, as we planned to do! Tom and I will take it in turns to keep guard in case anybody should come. But no one will."

Tom, tired out with all his adventures, was asleep at once, Andy sat beside him, covered in rugs, on guard.

CHAPTER ELEVEN

A Night on the Boat

It was a lovely night, with clouds going across the moon. The water was calm in the quiet cove and the boat hardly stirred. Andy puzzled over everything that had happened. Tom had said that boxes and crates were stored in one of the caves.

"How did the men get them there?" he wondered. Surely they couldn't have taken them up that steep cliff, through the waterfall opening, and down the winding passages that Tom described? That was quite impossible. Could a motor-boat get up that rushing underground river? No, the current was much too strong.

The puzzle was too difficult to solve and Andy soon gave up trying. After three hours he woke Tom. He was soon sitting up straight, the rugs well wrapped round him, looking out on the moonlit cove.

"Wake me in three hours, Tom," said

Andy, snuggling down in the rugs. It was a chilly night.

Tom felt terribly sleepy. He found that his head was nodding and his eyes were closing. And that would never do!

"I'd better walk about a bit," said Tom to himself. He carefully wriggled out of his rugs and paced the deck. He thought he heard a movement down below, and he opened the cabin hatch softly.

"Are you all right down there?" he said in a whisper.

Pippa's voice answered him. "I can't go to sleep, Tom, I've tried and tried. I just can't. Let me come up on deck with you and keep watch. I'm sure Andy wouldn't mind. I'll bring up some chocolate."

Chocolate sounded pretty good to Tom. He called back softly. "Well, don't wake Zoe. Come on up and bring your rug."

Pippa came up into the moonlight and looked round.

"Oh, isn't it lovely up here with the moonlight making the sea all silvery. What black shadows there are in Smugglers' Rock! I wonder if we'll have time to explore it tomorrow."

They sat down together, cuddling into the thick rugs. They munched the chocolate, which tasted delicious, eaten in the middle of the night! Tom felt wide awake now. He and Pippa began to discuss the day's happenings in low tones.

Then Tom put his hand in his pocket and pulled out the little red pearl button. "Look," he said. "I forgot about this. I found it on the floor of the cave behind the waterfall. That's what made me feel certain the hairy-legged man must hide somewhere in the cliff. After all, a button means a shirt or a jacket, doesn't it?"

"Was he wearing a red shirt when you saw him?" asked Pippa, turning the button over in her hand.

"No. I don't think so," said Tom. "I don't think the other fellow was, either. He was dressed like a fisherman."

The two fell silent for a while, enjoying the motion of the little boat and the noise that the water made against her.

Pippa yawned. "I think I'll go back now. I feel sleepy. I don't think anything will happen tonight, Tom. We're quite safe here."

She went below. Tom had no fear of falling asleep now. He felt wide awake. He looked at Smugglers' Rock. What a tall, steep, rocky place it was! The moon went behind a cloud. At once the rock became dark and black. Tom glanced idly at the top of it, and then he straightened himself up.

"There's a light up there!" he said under his breath. "Yes, there it is again. Flash, flash, flash! Somebody's signalling."

Tom shook Andy roughly. The boy awoke at once and sat up in alarm, not

knowing what to expect.

"Look, Andy, look, there's a light flashing at the very top of Smugglers' Rock!" said Tom. "I think it's a signal of some sort."

Andy looked. It went on flashing for some time and then stopped.

"What do you make of that?" said Tom.

"I don't know," said Andy. "Another puzzle! Anyway, I'm determined to get home as soon as possible tomorrow to report what's happening. I don't like this at all!"

The light did not flash any more. Andy looked at his watch, and then curled himself up. "I've got another hour of sleep," he said. "But wake me if you see anything else."

But nothing else happened in the rest of Tom's watch, much to his disappointment. He woke Andy up at the right time, and then curled up again in the rugs himself.

At dawn Andy woke them all. "We'll have a quick breakfast and then start off as soon as we can," he said.

"Which way are we going back?" asked Tom.

"I'm not sure," said Andy. "If I were certain that the motor-boat had gone, I'd risk the way we know. I've no idea if we can get out to sea from here, or what course to take if we can. I wish I dared climb up Smugglers' Rock to have a look out."

"Well, why shouldn't you?" said Tom.

"Have you forgotten those lights we saw flashing last night?" said Andy. "There's somebody on the island. It seems as if there is a network of people in this part of the coast!"

"But it's so early in the morning," said Tom. "No one will be about. Let's hop across to Smugglers' Rock after breakfast, climb up to that high point and quickly have a look out."

"Perhaps we'd better," said Andy. "Maybe no one will be about yet, as you say."

They sat down on the deck to have a good breakfast. This time it was hot soup with bread, and biscuits spread with marmalade. They drank hot cocoa, sweetened with condensed milk.

After eating, Andy glanced up the steep rocks of the island. "I think that high point that Tom thought would be a good one is about the best to choose," he said.

Soon they were clambering over the shining rocks, going up as fast as they could. There were no steep cliffs as there were before, just masses of rocks. From the high point there was a wonderful view. Andy scanned the sea with his hawk-like eyes.

"Nothing there," said Andy, pleased. "Good thing too, because I can't see another way to escape than the one we know."

"Let's get back home as quick as we can," said Zoe, and began to leap from rock to rock downwards. Andy tried to warn her, but it was too late. Zoe slipped and fell. Andy hurried to her in great alarm. Whatever had she done?

CHAPTER TWELVE

A HORRIBLE SHOCK

Zoe was sitting, pale-faced, on a rock, nursing one of her ankles. Tears ran down her cheeks.

"What's up?" asked Andy, kneeling down beside her.

"Oh, Andy, my ankle hurts," she wailed. "I'm a baby to cry, but I can't help it."

Andy took off Zoe's shoe. The ankle was already swollen. "I don't think it's a real sprain," he said. "You've just given it an awful twist. It will be all right soon."

"Pull her near this pool," said Tom, seeing a big, clear pool of rainwater in the hollow of a rock. "She can put her foot into it."

Zoe's foot felt better in the cold water. Soon the colour came back to her face and she rubbed away her tears. Andy thought she had better wait a while before trying to walk. He tried not to look worried. He really wanted to get home quickly.

Andy looked down the steep stretch of rocks below, leading to the cove where the boat was. He could not see the boat, but it was quite a distance below. It wouldn't be much good trying to help Zoe down at the moment. She would probably slip and fall again, dragging him with her. They must all wait in patience.

The children looked around them. Smugglers' Rock was a desolate-looking place. The island rose to a steep pinnacle. Anyone at the very top would have a perfectly marvellous view.

"I wish I could go right to the top," said Tom longingly.

"You won't do anything of the sort!" said Andy sharply. "I'm not having you get into any more trouble!"

"All right, all right," said Tom. "I only just said I'd *like* to go up there. I'm not going."

It seemed a long time till Zoe was able to put her foot to the ground without too much pain. She had twisted her ankle very badly.

"If you feel you can limp down now, Zoe,

with Tom and me helping you, we'd better go," said Andy.

Zoe tried her foot. Yes, she thought she could manage.

They started down. It was a slow little procession that went down, taking the very easiest way so that Zoe would not have to do any jumping. Twice she had to sit down and rest, but they got down to the cove at last. There lay the boat, rocking gently where they had left her. But something was lacking.

"Where's the sail?" said Tom. "Where is it?" Andy said nothing. He went jumping down to the cove and leaped on board the *Andy*. He did a quick search and then turned to the others with a grim face as they came aboard after him.

"Somebody's taken not only our sail, but our *oars* too!"

The three stared at him in horror.

"But, Andy, we can't go home now," said Zoe, looking pale with shock and pain.

"I'm afraid not," said Andy. "Someone came along while we were up on that high point. Someone who meant to keep us here."

Zoe began to cry again. Her ankle was hurting, and she was longing to get back home and be comforted by her mother. Andy put his arm round her.

"You go into the cabin and lie down," he said.

Zoe managed to get down into the cabin. She was glad to lie down on the little bunk and put her foot up. Pippa wrung a bandage out in cold seawater, and wrapped it carefully round the swelling.

The boys sat up on deck and talked gravely together.

"Those men chose this lonely, forgotten

bit of coast for whatever it is they wanted to do," said Andy. "And now we've butted in and spoiled their little game. It's clear they don't mean us to get home and talk about it. They'll keep us prisoner here till they've finished their job. Your mother and my father will be very anxious when we don't turn up."

"Well, they know where we've gone," said Tom, brightening up. "They'll come and look for us. Your father will get your uncle's boat and come and see what's happened. He's sure to come to Smugglers' Rock if he doesn't find us at the Cliff of Birds."

"But I bet our captors have thought of that," said Andy, grimly. "If they see Dad's boat, they'll take steps to see we're not about!"

Tom looked scared. "What about our boat?" he said. "They can't hide that."

Andy swallowed, and blinked back an unexpected tear. "Well, idiot," he said, trying to speak naturally, "they'll probably scuttle my boat, that's all! That's the best way to hide a boat you don't want found. I think they're pretty desperate fellows, and they won't mind sinking a boat if it suits them."

Tom stared at Andy in horror. "Oh, Andy," he said, and couldn't think of anything else to say at all. "Oh, Andy."

They said nothing for a few minutes. Then they heard Pippa coming up to soak Zoe's bandage again. "Don't tell the girls what we're afraid will happen," said Andy in a low voice.

"Right," said Tom. He gave Pippa a grin. "How's Zoe?"

"She says her ankle feels better now her foot is up," said Pippa. "We've been talking about the oars and the sail, Tom. Couldn't we go and look for them? We might find them hidden somewhere."

"Not very likely," said Andy. "It was smart work by the person who came along and saw our boat. He went off with them at once."

"I feel hungry," said Tom.

"Well, we should all eat something now," said Andy. "It's about twelve o'clock. Look at the sun!"

They had a good meal, and Andy and Tom kept a look out in case anyone was stealing about. But they saw no one.

"We must imagine we might be here for a while," said Andy. "I think we should remove all the food and rugs and things from the boat and find a good home in a cave or somewhere on Smugglers' Rock."

"Almost as if we'd been wrecked!" said Pippa, feeling suddenly cheerful. "That sort of thing is fun, even if we *are* in trouble! Come on. Let's find a good place."

CHAPTER THIRTEEN

A GOOD HOME

The three of them set off, leaving Zoe on deck because even though her ankle was much better, it was still painful. They went over the rugged rocks, keeping the *Andy* in sight all the time. The boys did not think anyone would go to the boat just then, but Andy was not going to risk leaving Zoe completely alone.

"It's no good going the way we went this morning," said Andy. "For one thing we can't see the boat from there, and for another I didn't spot a single place where we could get comfort and shelter. Did you?"

"No," said Tom. "It all looked very windswept. Let's go the other way. We must try and find a good spot higher up. If a storm came, I reckon that the sea would sweep right over these rocks we're on now."

"Yes, it would," said Andy. "I hope a storm doesn't come! That would about finish the *Andy*, lying there among those rocks. She'd be torn from her anchor and smashed to bits."

"Well, it doesn't look as if a storm is near," said Tom, not liking this conversation at all. "Look, Andy, let's climb up to that broad ledge. It looks like there's a cave behind it."

There was a cave; rather an awkward one with a very low roof at the front, so that the children had to crawl in almost flat. But inside it opened out. It smelled clean and fresh, and had a sandy floor.

"This'll do," Andy said, switching on his torch and looking round. "We can make the opening bigger by pulling away some of those overhanging tufts of roots, and burrowing down in the sand below. It will be rather fun lying inside and squinting out through that narrow opening at the sea."

"We've got an amazing view," said Pippa, and she lay down to peep out. "I can see the *Andy* from here. Zoe's still sitting on deck. And look, you can see the Cliff of Birds and make out the channel between the two ridges of rocks too."

"We could see anyone coming to rescue us!" said Tom. "Couldn't we, Andy? If we saw your father's boat, we could signal!"

There was a rocky ledge at one side of the cave. Pippa patted it. "This will do to put our stores on," she said. "And we'll put our cushions and rugs on the sandy floor. We shall be very snug here. If only Mummy knew where we are!"

"Let's go back and get our stores," said Andy. "Come on, Tom."

They all squeezed out. Andy looked up at the top edge of the entrance. He began to pull away some of the earth and roots that hung down from above. Soon he had made the entrance a little bigger.

"That will let more air in," he said. "It might be stuffy at night, but it will certainly be warm!"

They went back to the boat and told Zoe all about it. She showed them her ankle.

"It's much better!" she said. "I could help to carry the things up."

"No, you must keep resting it," said Andy. "We'll take the things up. You can be in charge of the boat."

They went down into the cabin and collected all the food. There was quite a lot! Zoe got the little paraffin stove and a kettle ready for them to take too. They would need to boil water for tea or cocoa.

Rugs, cushions, fishing tackle, the cabin lamp, mugs, plates, everything was stripped from the fishing boat. The girls, not knowing what the boys were afraid of, were astonished to see everything being taken. Pippa thought it was most unnecessary.

"Why are we taking so much?" she grumbled. "I'm tired! Andy, it's silly to take everything!"

"Do as your skipper tells you!" said Tom.

"You're a good one to talk!" snapped Pippa.

"I'll finish carrying the things then, Pippa," said Andy. "You go back to Zoe and give her some help coming up."

By teatime the cave was well stocked. When Zoe arrived, she was delighted. The only thing was that it was rather dark there, and Andy did not want to use their torches more than was necessary.

"We could light the cabin lamp," said Zoe.

"There's not a great deal of paraffin," said Andy. "We'll only light that when it's really dark, at night. We can just manage to see, if nobody stops up the entrance with his body! Tom, get out of the way. You're blocking our daylight!"

"I was just having a look around," said Tom.

"I suppose Andy's father will rescue us tomorrow," said Zoe. "It's a pity really, because it's such fun sleeping in a cave."

"Do you suppose the people who stole our oars and sail know we've come here?" said Pippa.

"I expect so," said Andy. "I'm sure

they've got look-outs posted. They must have seen us down in the cove early this morning and been very surprised."

"How annoyed they must have been," said Tom. "We've butted in at just the wrong time."

The little kettle was now boiling on the stove, making a nice gurgling sound. Zoe cut some bread and butter, and put out a jar of plum jam.

"We'd better not have tins of meat or sardines, had we?" she said to Andy. "Just in case we aren't rescued tomorrow."

"Yes," said Andy. "We must go slow on the food for a while."

Even though he was worried about what might happen to his boat, Andy couldn't help enjoying his tea. The paraffin stove was making the cave very warm, so the children went and sat out on the ledge in the sunshine. A beautiful view spread before them.

"Rocks, and sea, and more rocks, and more sea, and sky and clouds and birds making a pattern in the air," said Zoe, munching her slice of bread and jam. "I like looking at things like that when I'm having a picnic. It makes my food taste nicer!"

"Look!" said Andy suddenly. "Someone is coming round the side of the cove! He's going to the *Andy*. Let's get back into the cave and watch!"

CHAPTER FOURTEEN

THE HUNT FOR THE CHILDREN

Hardly breathing, the four children looked down into the cove and saw the man walking over the rocks towards the *Andy*. He was tall and dark, with a black beard. He looked like a fisherman, and he had big sea boots on.

"Do you know him, Andy?" whispered Tom.

Andy shook his head. "No. He doesn't come from our district. Look, he's getting into the boat."

A faint shout came up to the children. "He's shouting to us to come out!" said Pippa. "He thinks we're still there!"

The man stood on the deck, waiting. But when no one answered, he opened the cabin hatch. He looked down and saw that the boat looked remarkably empty of goods as well as of crew!

"He's found out that we've removed all

our things!" said Andy.

"Look, there's another man now," whispered Tom. "Doesn't he look odd?"

He did. He was bandy-legged and walked as though he sat on a horse. He had on sea boots and an oilskin that flapped in the wind. He had gingery hair and he was yelling to the other man.

"Now they're talking about our disappearance," said Tom, quite enjoying himself. "Do you think they'll come to find us, Andy? We're well hidden here."

The men went off in different directions. It was plain that they were hunting for the children. They peeped about the cove, and occasionally shouted, though the children couldn't hear the words.

"Shouting to us to come out, I suppose," said Tom.

The men came up a bit higher, and looked around the rocks. There were one or two places where the children might have hidden.

Now they could hear what the men were shouting. "Where are those brats?" yelled the bandy-legged man. "Wait till I find them! Wasting my time like this!"

The children lay quite quiet.

"We'd better go right into the cave," said Andy. "If they come any higher they might catch sight of us."

So they wriggled back until they could only catch a glimpse of the sea through the entrance. The sound of footsteps was coming near.

"There's a cave somewhere about here!" they heard the bandy-legged man call. "Maybe they've gone there."

"Well, take a look then," said the dark man, and his steps came nearer. The children saw his feet pass the entrance! Their hearts almost stopped beating with fright. But the feet went right past and out of sight.

Then they saw the bandy legs of the other man going by too. But just as he was passing the legs stopped.

"I'm sure that cave was here," said his rather hoarse voice. "Wait, what's this!" His foot kicked into the entrance of the cave. Then he bent down and looked inside, finding it very awkward indeed. But he could see nothing, of course, for it was pitch-black inside.

"No one surely could creep in there!" said the voice of the dark man. "Look, there's a cave higher up. Maybe they're in that."

To the children's relief the bandy-legged man moved on. They breathed more easily but did not dare to move. They heard more shouting and calling and then there was silence.

"Is it safe to peep out and see where they are?" said Tom, who was longing to know what was happening.

"No," said Andy. "They may be sitting quietly somewhere waiting for us to show ourselves."

They all kept very still and quiet. Then they heard the voices again. The dark man sounded thoroughly exasperated.

"I tell you, Sandy, we must find these children. They know too much!"

"You can see for yourself they aren't here," said the other, sounding sulky. "They've taken all their things and maybe gone to the other side."

"I hope not!" said the other man. "They'll certainly fall into trouble there! No, they've not gone far. They couldn't carry so many things very far."

The men were standing near the cave again now. The children heard the dark man suddenly give an exclamation.

"Look!" he said. "Spots of oil! Who could have spilled it but those children? They took the lamp and the little cooking stove out of the cabin, so maybe it was from one of those."

"It looks as if they must be in that cave then, after all!" said the bandy-legged man. "Little pests, to give us so much trouble. I'll strike a match and look in the cave."

"He'll see us now," whispered Andy. "You leave everything to me. I'll manage this."

Then the bandy-legged man knelt down and looked with difficulty into the low, ground-level entrance. He struck a match, and held its flame inside the entrance. He gave a loud cry.

"Hey! Here they are, the whole lot of them, lying as quiet as mice! Come on out, all of you!"

The children said nothing. The match went out. The man lit another and this time the man with the beard knelt down and

looked into the entrance, his head almost on the ground. He saw the children too. He spoke to them with authority.

"Now, come out! We won't hurt you. Come along."

"We're not coming," said Andy.

There was a silence. Then the bandy-legged man began to lose his temper. "Look here, you, you—"

"That's enough, Sandy," said the dark man. He called into the cave, "How many of you are there?"

"Four," said Andy. "And let me warn you that the first man who wriggles in here will get a blow on the head with the stove!"

"That's no way to talk," said the dark man after a moment's pause. "We're not going to hurt you. We want to take you somewhere more comfortable."

"We couldn't be more comfortable than we are, thanks," said Andy politely.

"Are you coming or have I got to come in and get you?" yelled Sandy suddenly.

"Come in, if you like," said Andy. "If you come in feet first we'll send you out double quick, with a good shove. And if you come in head first, we've got the stove waiting!"

"Leave them, Sandy," said the dark man, standing up. "It'll be worse for them when they do come out. We can always get them out when we want to."

"Well, we'll want them out as soon as we sight anything," said Sandy, standing up too. "Better give me your orders."

"We can leave them for tonight," said the dark man, and began to walk away. "We have other things to do!"

Soon there was silence again. It was getting darker in the cave, for the sun had gone, and twilight was coming. The children lay still for some time. Finally Andy crawled to the entrance and peered out.

"Can't see into the cove," he said. "Too dark. Can't see any sign of those men, either. Brutes!"

"You wouldn't really drop the stove on that man's head, would you?" asked Zoe, horrified at the thought.

"No," said Andy. "But I thought the threat might keep them out of here till tomorrow, when I hope my dad will arrive. Then we'll creep out and yell for all we're worth!"

"That's what those men were afraid we'll do," said Tom. He yawned. "I feel sleepy. One of us will have to be on guard during the night. We don't want anyone surprising us."

"Zoe and I will take turns tonight too," said Pippa. "You boys didn't get much sleep last night. Can't we rig up a pile of tins at the entrance, so that anyone trying to creep in would knock them over?"

"Jolly good idea, Pippa," said Andy. "We'll do that at once. I feel as sleepy as

Tom does. You can have the first watch, me the next, Zoe the next, and Tom the next. Where are the tins? I can't see in this darkness!"

Pippa lit the lamp, and the cave at once glowed with warm yellow light. It seemed cosy and snug in there. The children wrapped rugs round themselves and put cushions at their heads. Pippa built a pile of tins at the entrance to the cave and sat bolt upright, proud to have the first watch.

Andy blew out the lamp. Darkness settled on the cave once more. Soon there was silence except for the peaceful breathing of three sleeping children. Pippa sat tense, holding her breath at every sound. She hoped that nobody would come while she was keeping watch!

CHAPTER FIFTEEN

PLENTY OF THINGS HAPPEN!

Pippa watched and listened until it was time to wake Andy. She felt quite worn out by the time she had been on guard for two hours. It seemed a very long time when everything was dark and still.

Andy had nothing to report when he woke Zoe. Zoe kept watch for two hours, feeling rather sleepy at times but keeping herself awake by reciting all the poetry she had ever learned.

Tom's turn came next. He was so sound asleep that Zoe thought she never would wake him! But at last she had him sitting up.

"You're to wake Andy in two hours' time, and he'll take the dawn watch," she said. "He says he doesn't mind, he'll have had plenty of sleep by then."

Tom couldn't keep his eyes open! He nearly yawned his head off. Then he felt hungry and wondered where the girls had put the chocolate. He groped around and found some on the little ledge where the food was stored. He tore the paper off the chocolate bar and munched away happily.

Nothing happened in Tom's watch. He woke Andy just before dawn. The boy sat up, and saw the first grey light filtering through the entrance. He wriggled over and looked out, but could see nothing at all.

When the sun rose the others awoke. Zoe sat up, stretching. She knew where she was at once, but Pippa didn't.

"Where am I?" she asked, sitting up, half frightened.

"Only in the cave, silly," said Zoe. "It's daylight again. Ooh, I do feel stiff. I'm a bit cold too."

Tom wriggled to the cave entrance for a breath of fresh air. He sniffed eagerly, and looked down to the cove. He gave such a loud cry that everyone jumped.

"What's up? What's the matter?" they cried.

"Our boat, it's gone!" cried Tom. "Look, the cove's quite empty!"

Andy scrambled out of the cave and

looked down into the cove. It was just as Tom said, the boat was gone. He didn't say a word. Tom knew how he was feeling.

"Oh, Andy, you don't think those men have sunk her, do you?" he said. "Surely nobody could do such a terrible thing!"

Andy still said nothing. He went and busied himself with lighting the stove and putting the kettle on.

"Poor Andy!" whispered Zoe, with tears in her eyes. "Why should those men sink our boat, Tom?"

"I suppose so that no one should guess we were here, if they came looking for us," said Tom. "You see, we've stumbled on some kind of secret, and those men don't want us to tell anyone what little we know!"

The girls looked scared. Then Zoe cheered up. "But when we see Andy's father's boat coming, we'll climb up to the high rocks and signal!"

"Kettle's boiling," came Andy's voice from the back. "Shall we have some cocoa?"

As they ate their breakfast, Andy still looked miserable. "Dad ought to be along soon," he said. "When we didn't come home last night, as we should have done, everyone would have been worried. Dad would start out for the Cliff of Birds early this morning. If he didn't find us there he'd come along here. We must keep a look out."

They finished breakfast. Andy wriggled out of the cave and peered down to the cove. "I'm just going to look to see if the poor old *Andy* is at the bottom there," he said. "I won't be long."

The others watched as he ran down the steep rocks and stood where the *Andy* had been anchored, peering down into the water.

"Look, there's that bandy-legged man again!" said Tom, suddenly. "And two others with him! They've seen Andy, but he's seen them too. Look at him leaping up the rocks! Oh, Andy, hurry, hurry!"

Andy was not afraid of being caught by the three men. He was far swifter than they were. He leaped up the rocks, and wriggled into the cave with plenty of time to spare.

"I don't know if they've come for us," he panted. "But they won't make us come out! I don't see how they can unless they wriggle in on their tummies, and they are at our mercy then!"

"Andy, did you see the boat?" asked Zoe anxiously.

Andy shook his head. "No, there's no sign of her. I think they must have taken her out to sea and scuttled her in really deep water."

"Look out," said Tom. "Here come the men."

There was the dark man, the bandy-legged man with the beard, and one that Tom recognised at once.

"Look, see the fisherman with the glasses on his nose? Well, that's one of the men I saw in the cave at the Cliff of Birds! How did he get here? Nasty-looking collection, aren't they?"

Andy felt desperate. He was angered by the disappearance of his boat, and quite ready to push any of the men down the rocks! If the men tried to wriggle into the cave, he was quite determined to fight with any weapon he could.

The three men came to the cave. The dark man called out to them. "Well, children, are you more sensible today? Are you coming out?"

No one said anything. The man called

124

again, impatiently. "Come along now! No one will hurt you! You'll be sorry if you don't come out voluntarily. We don't want to make you come!"

Still no reply. There was a short silence, and the dark man gave a rapid order.

"Set it going, Sandy."

Sandy put something down by the cave just within the entrance. It looked like some sort of can. The children watched in silence. Sandy struck a match and held it to something in the can. It flared up. The man seemed to damp it down and, instead of flames, smoke came out.

The wind blew the thick, billowing smoke into the cave. Tom got a smell of it first and he coughed.

"The beasts!" said Andy suddenly. "They're trying to smoke us out of the cave, like hunters do wild animals."

The smoke poured in. The children coughed. It was quite harmless, but the children didn't know that. They felt frightened.

"It's no good. We'll have to go out," spluttered Andy. "Keep close to me, and do exactly what I say. Don't be afraid."

Before he went out, Andy felt along the ledge for a packet of salt he knew was there. He tore it open, and poured the salt into his pocket. Then, panting and coughing, he crawled out of the cave. The girls came next, and then Tom. The men stared at them.

"Why, they're only kids, except for this fisher boy," said Sandy. "Interfering little varmints!"

"Look! Look, Andy! There's your

father's boat!" cried Tom, suddenly, and they all swung round. Sure enough, away in the distance was a big fishing boat.

"Hurray!" yelled Tom. "We're all right. You'll have to let us go now! There's Andy's father."

"Blindfold them and take them away," said the dark man, to the children's dismay. "There's no time to lose!"

The men pushed them forward roughly and they stumbled over a rocky path. Where were they going? And why were they blindfolded? Were they going to some secret hideout that no one must know the way to?

"Oh," wept Pippa. "Let us go, please let us go!"

But the men pushed them forward roughly, and when Andy's father sailed into the cove, there was no one to be seen!

CHAPTER SIXTEEN

PRISONERS!

Andy was doing his best to try and memorise the way, as they went along. "Up all the time, to the left first and then fairly straight, then a steep bit up, where they had to help us, then to the left again, keeping inwards. I suppose we are behind big rocks now, so that no one can see us from the sea."

Andy was doing something else too, that he hoped his captors were not noticing! He was dropping little pinches of salt along the way! If ever he got free he hoped that he might be able to follow the trail of salt to the hiding place!

"I hope it doesn't rain!" thought Andy. "If it rains, the salt will melt."

After about ten minutes, the men told the children to halt. There was a pause. Andy tried to pull off his blindfold, but he got a hard clip on the ear at once. He heard a puzzling grating noise. Then the children were pushed roughly forward again, and it seemed darker through their blindfolds.

"Going into the island itself," thought Andy. They went upwards again, and Andy cautiously put his hands out to the side of him. He felt rocky walls each side. They were in a passage!

At last they all came to a stop. "You'll be safe here!" said the jeering voice of the bandy-legged man, and he stripped off their blindfolds. They blinked. They were standing in a high-roofed place, looking at a big door. Andy felt something bright at the back of him and swung round. He gave a gasp.

They were in a very high cave that opened on to the sunlit sea. It lay very far below. There was an absolutely sheer drop down from the cave to the sea. A terrifying drop!

There was a bang as the heavy wooden door behind them shut. The children heard bolts being shot into place. They were prisoners, but what a strange prison! They all gazed out of the opening. But there was nothing to be seen except a dangerous, treacherous, rock-strewn shore, where waves battered themselves into foam and spray.

"It's said that it's too dangerous to sail around the island beyond a certain point," said Andy. "We must be almost on the other side of it now. I doubt my father could get here."

"I bet those men knew we couldn't possibly signal from here," said Tom gloomily. "Beasts!"

"I hope they're not going to keep us here long," said Andy. "I don't fancy being shut up like this, without any food or rugs."

The children sat down in the cave. For about three hours nothing happened. They gazed out to sea, hoping to see a boat or a ship they could signal to, but not one came into sight. Then they heard the door being unbolted. They all sat up. Who was it? It was Sandy. He was carrying a big jug of water and a plate of bread and meat.

"You don't deserve a thing!" he said in his rather hoarse voice. "Interfering, tiresome nuisances you are! Eat this, and be glad of it!"

"How long do you plan to keep us here?" asked Andy. "And what have you done with my boat?"

"Why? Are you thinking of trying to sail away?" asked Sandy, with a nasty smile. "You can give up all hope of that! She's sunk!"

Andy turned away, sick at heart.

"Serves you right. Children that come

sticking their noses into what isn't their business deserve all they get," said Sandy, who seemed to enjoy being nasty. "Maybe you'll be here for weeks!"

He went out and shut the door, bolting it noisily. "Bah!" they heard him say again outside.

The bread was stale and hard, and the meat tasted a bit musty, but it made them feel a little better. They did not feel very cheerful as they gazed out through the opening at the sea and the sky, thinking that they might be there for weeks.

Andy tried to cheer them up. "He was only trying to scare us all," he told them. "He'll let us out as soon as my father's boat has gone away. Don't worry!"

Towards five o'clock, when they were all feeling very hungry, they heard the bolts of the door being pulled back. This time it was the dark man who came in. He spoke to them in his deep voice, and they again heard his slightly foreign accent.

"You can go now. The ship that has been hunting for you has gone. But if it is sighted again, you will have to come here once more."

"Why all this mystery and fuss?" asked Andy. "What are you doing that you want to hide?"

"Children shouldn't ask dangerous questions!" said the man, and his eyes gleamed angrily.

Once again, the children's eyes were bound tightly, and Sandy and the dark man took them out of the cave. Downwards they went, and then came out into the open air. They were taken some way over the rocks, and then the blindfolds were stripped off.

They blinked. "We're near the cove!" said Tom. "Good. Let's go up to our cave and get a meal. I'm really hungry."

Andy watched to see which way the men went. "If only I knew what they are doing!" he said, in a low voice. "Well, I'll find the way into the heart of the island, and discover what's going on!"

"But how can you?" said Tom. "We'd never find the way!"

The children went and looked at their larder hungrily.

"What shall we have? Let's go mad and have something good," said Zoe. "What about a tin of ham? We could heat up a tin of peas to go with it. And a tin of pineapple chunks afterwards."

"With condensed milk," said Pippa. "And we'll make cocoa too."

They had a most delicious meal, and ate every single thing they had prepared, and drank the last drop from the cocoa jug. As Pippa put back the mugs, she noticed the salt was missing.

"Where's the salt gone?" she asked in surprise.

"I took it!" said Andy. "And I'll tell you why! I poured it into my pocket, and dropped out pinches of salt as we went along this morning. Now I will be able to find the way into the depths of the island, by following my trail!"

"Oh, Andy, what a brilliant idea!" said Tom. "Let's go now and see if we can find the trail. Come on quickly! What a clever thing to do! We'll go and spy on those men this evening!"

CHAPTER SEVENTEEN

A Trail to Follow

Tom, Zoe and Pippa thought it was very exciting to have a salt trail to follow. But Andy looked up at the sky in alarm. There were rainclouds.

"Blow, blow, blow!" he said.

"Are you talking to the wind, or just being annoyed?" asked Zoe.

"I'm being annoyed," said Andy, as he felt the first drop of rain on his cheek. "The rain will melt my trail!"

"Well, let's hurry then, before it begins to pour!" said Tom, and they scuttled down the rocks. They saw a pinch of salt.

"Here's one! We passed by here. And there's another! Come on, we can easily spot the white grains!" They followed the salt trail for a little way up the rocks, and round to the left. Then the rain came down properly, and in a flash the salt disappeared! Andy looked very gloomy.

"Just my luck! Why didn't I follow the trail straightaway? And why didn't I think of something more sensible to use than salt?"

"Never mind, Andy," said Zoe. "It was a really good idea, anyway!"

"I bet your father won't give up hunting for us yet, Andy," said Tom. "He'll be along again tomorrow. If so, those men will take us to that cave again. We can lay another trail then."

"But not with salt," said Zoe. "Let's think of something else."

"It must be something the men don't notice," said Pippa. "What can it be?"

Nobody could think of anything for some time. Then Tom had a brainwave. "I know! Do you remember seeing those little pink shells down in the cove? Well, what about filling our pockets with them? No one would notice shells, they're so usual by the sea. They would make a lovely trail to follow!"

"Good idea, Tom," said Andy. "We'll do that. We could collect them now, then we'd have them ready in case the men take us off to that cave again tomorrow."

So they all hunted for the little pink shells in the cove and filled their pockets. It wouldn't matter in the least if the men found the shells, because children always collect them. It began to grow dark.

"Better go back to our cave," said Andy. "We'll light the lamp and have a cosy evening. We'll make some tea and have biscuits for supper – if Tom hasn't eaten them all yet."

They went up to their cave and squeezed in. Andy lit the lamp and the stove too, so that they could boil the kettle. The cave was soon warm and cosy.

"This is nice," said Zoe, pulling a rug round her. "I know horrid things have happened, and I hate to think of people being worried about us, but I can't help enjoying being in this cave, feeling warm and dry, and having ginger biscuits to nibble."

Everyone felt the same, though Andy looked rather stern and thoughtful. Zoe knew he was always thinking of his lost boat.

They slept well that night and no one kept watch because there didn't seem to be any need to. They didn't feel that the men would harm them and they all wanted a good night's sleep. So they slept soundly, and woke when the sun was quite high.

Andy was surprised. "We're late this morning!" he said.

"Andy! The men are coming again!" said Tom, peering out of the cave. "And, oh wow, look over there! One . . . two . . . three . . . four . . . *five* fishing boats! Your father's got half the fleet out looking for us!"

"Let's signal, quick!" cried Andy. But the boats were too far away to see them, and at that moment the same three men as before came up to the cave.

"Remember the shells," said Andy in a low voice.

"Come out, all of you," said the dark man's voice. Tom had scrambled back, so they were all in the cave now.

"We'll go out without making a fuss," said Andy to the others. "We don't want to be smoked out again. That was horrid."

They squeezed out of the cave and stood up. The men blindfolded them quickly. Then once more they were pushed along until they were in the same cave as before, looking out to sea from a great height, and they heard the wooden door being bolted behind them.

"I dropped my . . ." began Zoe in an eager voice, and broke off with a groan as Tom and Andy poked her sharply. "Don't! What did you do that for?"

Andy nodded his head towards the door. "You don't know if any of them are behind, listening to what we might say," he whispered. "Don't say anything till I nod my head at you."

They stayed silent for a while. Then, when Andy was certain their captors had gone, he nodded his head. "But speak low," he said.

"I dropped my shells all the way," whispered Zoe. "I haven't a single one left!"

"I've dropped all mine too," said Pippa. "I was so afraid the men would notice. Did you drop yours, Tom?"

"Of course," said Tom.

"I've got about four left," said Andy. "I was afraid I'd drop them all before we got here, and that would be sickening!"

"Well, we seem to have done all right between us," said Tom. "We ought to be able to track down the trail here easily enough."

"I think we'll have to do it at night," said Andy. "The men will be about in the daytime, but at night I imagine they sleep."

"Oooh, at night?" said Zoe. "I wouldn't like that!"

"Well, you don't have to go," said Andy. "Tom and I will leave you and Pippa cosily asleep in the cave. We'll take your torches too, then we shall have plenty of light."

After a while Sandy arrived with dry bread and meat. This time it was ham, which tasted a lot nicer. Then, sooner than the day before, they were set free.

"I think your friends will now give up the search for you!" said the dark man in rather a nasty voice. "You will be free to roam on the island. But you will find that steep, sheer rocks make it impossible to get round to the other side, so do not try. You may fall and be hurt, and if so, we shall not help you."

"What kind people you are!" remarked Andy. Sandy looked as if he would like to punch him, but he didn't. The men went off and left them alone.

Zoe ran a little way up the rocks as soon as they were out of sight. She came back, her face pink with excitement.

"Our trail of shells is there, quite easy to see! You'll be able to follow them well, Tom and Andy. They stretch up over the rocks," said Zoe. "I can see it for quite a long way!"

"Well, I hope the men don't spot it then," said Andy. "We'll do a bit of tracking tonight, Tom. It *will* be exciting!"

CHAPTER EIGHTEEN

A Strange Midnight Journey

The boys thought they would start following the trail at midnight. They decided to try and go to sleep for a few hours, so that they would not be too tired.

"I'll keep awake, and wake you at midnight, if you like," said Zoe.

"No. It's all right. I'll wake up," said Andy. "We can all go to sleep."

So they cuddled up in their rugs, put their heads down on the cushions and were soon asleep and dreaming. At midnight, just as he had said he would, Andy awoke. He sat up and switched on his torch. He shook Tom hard and woke him.

"Wh-what!" said Tom and woke with a jump.

"Shh! Don't wake the girls!" whispered Andy.

"Give me Zoe's torch," whispered Tom. "My battery's getting low."

Andy handed it to him. Then the boys squeezed out of the cave and stood on the windy hill. It was cold and dark.

"Now to pick up the trail!" said Andy, and shone his torch down, shading it with his fingers so as not to show too much light.

The boys soon picked up the trail of pink shells, which gleamed brightly in the torchlight. They made their way over the rocks, following the shells easily. There was one bit where the trail broke and they went wrong, but they soon came back and found the right way.

"We must all have stopped dropping shells at the same moment!" said Tom. "But it wasn't much of a gap. Come on."

They went on and on, round to the left and upwards. Then the trail of shells suddenly stopped.

"This is where we must have gone inside," said Andy and he shone his torch on the rocks that towered beside him. But there was no entrance into the hill. The wall of rock stood unbroken.

"Funny!" said Andy. "Perhaps the trail goes on after all. Perhaps we've come to a gap again, where none of us threw down shells! I'll go on and see. You stay here and shine your torch out now and again, so that I shall know where to come back to."

He soon came back. "There's no more to be seen," he said. "This *must* be where we went in. But how can anyone walk through solid rock?"

He shone his torch on the rocky wall again. He discovered a narrow crack that seemed to go inside the hill.

"Funny!" said Andy again, and shone his torch up and down the crack. "Look, Tom, this crack seems the only way into the hill, but how could anyone squeeze through it? We certainly didn't!"

Then Andy remembered something.

"Do you remember the funny noise we heard?" he asked Tom. "A sort of grating noise? I wonder if by any chance this rock moves."

Andy shone his torch down on the crack again. Then he shone it above and below, and found something on the ledge below that almost made him shout.

"Look, Tom, an iron bar! It must be put there to use as a lever! Well, I'll try!"

He picked up the iron bar and slipped it into the crack. He and Tom pressed hard, and lo and behold, part of the rock slipped aside with a curious grating noise! It was balanced so finely on its base that it could be moved almost at a touch. Now it was open, the boys saw the dark entrance into the hill. Andy shone his torch in.

"Well, who would have thought of a way in like that!" he said in a whisper. "We won't shut the rock behind us, in case we can't open it from the inside. We don't want to make ourselves prisoners."

He put down the iron bar and went inside the hill. A long tunnel yawned in front of them. After they had followed it for some way it split in two. One tunnel went upwards and the other downwards. Which should they follow?

"Up, I think," said Andy. "It may lead us to the light at the top of the island and we could have a good look at it."

The boys crept on up the tunnel, using their torches, but switching them off at once if they thought they heard anything. The tunnel split into two again. One tunnel ran on the level and the other still went up.

Andy and Tom went along the level one to see what they could find. They came to a strong wooden door, with bolts and a lock.

"I bet this is the door of the cave those men shut us in today and yesterday," said Andy. "We'll see, shall we?"

Cautiously they opened the door. Yes, it was the same cave. They retraced their steps and joined the tunnel that went on upwards.

Suddenly they saw a light shining somewhere in front of them.

"Quiet!" hissed Andy. "Stand still and listen."

But there was nothing to be heard. They went on cautiously and came to an enormous cave lit by a great ship's lantern. This cave was furnished most comfortably, with two or three mattresses, a table, chairs, and store cupboards. A stove was burning, with a kettle boiling away on top. A very good meal was spread out on the table, which made Tom feel very hungry. Pink slices of ham lay on a dish, and a tin of corned beef had been opened. A fruitcake stood on a plate, and there was a tin of peaches.

"Look at that!" said Tom, his mouth watering, "I really must have a slice of that ham!"

"Be careful!" whispered Andy. "The meal is set for someone and the kettle is boiling, so the man it's meant for will be back soon! We don't want to be caught."

"Can't we just nip in and get some of the ham?" begged Tom.

"Well, quick then!" said Andy. They darted in. The boys snatched four slices of the ham, and half a loaf of bread. Andy cut an enormous slice of cake. They stuffed everything into their pockets and were just about to run out of the cave when they heard someone coming!

"Quick! Hide!" said Andy, looking round. "Into that chest, quick!"

They lifted the lid of an enormous chest and got inside it, putting the lid down quietly just as Sandy came into the lit cave. He came in singing lustily, and took the kettle off the stove.

He made himself some tea, and then sat down to the table. He stared at the ham.

"Look at that! Where's half the ham gone? And where's my bread? If that greedy pig Jake has come in here and taken my supper again, I'll knock him down!" Sandy growled. Then he saw that someone had cut a huge slice of the fruitcake and he rose to his feet in anger.

"My cake too! I'll teach him! I'll punch him till he can't tell if he's standing up or sitting down. I'll . . . I'll . . ."

He disappeared out of the cave, taking the tunnel that led downwards. Andy and Tom wanted to laugh. Poor Jake! He would deny he had taken Sandy's supper till he was blue in the face, but Sandy wouldn't believe him.

"Let's get out of here while we've got the chance," said Andy. "We'd better go upwards, or we shall run into Sandy. Come on."

Tom stopped to snatch a few more bits of ham and another piece of cake. Then he ran after Andy into the tunnel. Soon they came to some rough steps cut in a steep upwards passage. It seemed as if they would never end. Tom gave a gasp and sat down.

"Andy, I must have a rest! These steps are so steep."

Andy sat beside him, panting too. He

smiled to think of Sandy going off to accuse Jake, whoever he might be, of taking his supper. The ham, bread and cake were now safely disposed of, and both boys felt very satisfied. Shortly they got up and continued on their way. Suddenly the steps stopped, and they came out on to a kind of platform. The wind swept around them viciously.

"We're on the top of Smugglers' Rock, where that light was flashed from!" cried Andy. "Wow, isn't the wind strong!"

Tom flashed his torch on to an enormous lamp, "Look, the beams from this would flash a long way, to ships far out, waiting to come in with smuggled goods!"

"That's just about right!" said Andy. "We're very high up here. Ships many miles away could catch these signals."

Suddenly he clutched Tom's arm. "Listen, aren't those footsteps, and whistling again? Hop under the platform that the lamp's on!"

Moments later Sandy entered and began to do something to the lamp. In a minute or two brilliant flashes lit up the night. The lamp was signalling to someone.

Sandy stayed for ten minutes. Then he

turned out the light and went down the steps again. The boys didn't dare to follow. They went down a few steps, found a rough, hidden corner in the rocky wall, and lay down there. In a few moments they were asleep!

They awoke at dawn, stiff and shivering, cross at having fallen asleep. Andy went on to the windy platform and looked all round. What a marvellous view. Why, he could see all round the rocky island!

He looked down on the side he had never seen before and gave a low cry. "Look, Tom, look down there! What do you make of that?"

CHAPTER NINETEEN

MORE DISCOVERIES

The boys gazed far, far down, to where the sea gleamed in the early sunlight. They saw a harbour; an almost round cove, protected on all sides by steep, rugged rocks. At first it seemed there was no outlet to the sea at all, so the harbour looked more like an inland lake.

The harbour was full of motor-boats, some large, some small! One of them was making its way into the cove through an opening so narrow that the boys could scarcely make it out.

"Look at that!" said Andy. "Who would dream this natural harbour was here! No one can see it from the other side of the island, and I imagine that unless you know your way among those rocks, you'd never find your way in. Well, well, a perfect little smugglers' haunt!"

"No wonder they knew when my father

was coming!" said Andy. "They could see his boat miles away! I wonder if they spotted ours, when we went to the Cliff of Birds."

"They did the second time," said Tom. "That's why they sent out that motor-boat to stop us!"

"You're right," said Andy. "Wow, what a huge operation this must be! I suppose they send those motor-boats out to ships lying at anchor some miles away, ships that have seen this signal, and take off their goods to bring them here to this wonderful hiding place."

"I suppose they smuggle stuff to save paying duty," said Tom. "But how do they get them away from here? There's no road overland even from the Cliff of Birds!"

"It's a real puzzle," said Andy.

"Do you remember I told you about all those boxes and crates in that cave in the Cliff of Birds?" said Tom. "How do you suppose they get them there from here?"

Andy couldn't answer him. The two boys stood looking out for some time, watching the motor-boats at rest, and seeing men unload the one that had just come in.

"I bet that boat went out last night to whatever ship Sandy was signalling to," said Andy, "and slipped back here before dawn."

"They must have men who know the rocks like the back of their hands," said Tom. "I wouldn't care to chug through them!"

"I think we'd better get back," said Andy. "The girls will be longing to know all we've seen!"

They turned to go down the steps. It was dark down there, but they did not like to switch on their torches in case Sandy was about and spotted them. They came to the big cave. Quietly Andy slid his head in to see if Sandy was there. Yes! He could hear him as well as see him! The bandy-legged man was lying on his back, fast asleep. His mouth was open and he was snoring loudly.

"There's no one else there," said Tom, looking round quickly. "And he hasn't finished that corned beef or the peaches. Let's get them."

"No, he might wake up," said Andy, pulling him back.

"He won't. He's snoring hard," said Tom.

"Come on. We haven't had any breakfast!"

He and Andy stole in quickly and snatched up the bowl of peaches and the corned beef. As they turned to go, Sandy gave such an enormous snore that he made Tom jump. The boy tripped over an uneven piece of rocky floor and fell headfirst. The bowl he was carrying smashed to pieces.

"Idiot!" hissed Andy, and dragged him up. They tore down the passage. But Sandy was wide awake now. He sat up and yelled:

"What, you came back again! After the pasting I gave you last night too! You greedy fellow, you pig, you . . ."

"Run! He thought we were the bloke that he sorted out last night!" gasped Andy. "Run! We'll hide somewhere before he catches us."

The boys fled down and down. They passed the forked tunnel that led to the cave where they had been held prisoner. They tore on, hoping soon to get to the place where the tunnel split in two.

"Once we get to that fork in the tunnel we'll be all right!" panted Andy. "We can slip out of the entrance and make our way back!"

But when they got to the end of the passage, the rock had been slid back into place! There was no way out.

"Bother! How do we open it from this side?" wondered Andy. He pushed and pulled and shoved, but the rock would not move. "It's no good. We can't open it."

"Well, we can't go back up the tunnel to Sandy's room," said Tom. "He'd be sure to catch us sooner or later."

"Let's go to where the tunnel forks and take the downward path," said Andy. "It might take us out another way."

So back they went once more, listening cautiously for Sandy. They took the downward fork and made their way along dark, musty passages, winding here and there.

"Listen, what's that?" said Tom.

It was the sound of a quarrel. The boys crept nearer to the shouts.

"It's Sandy going for Jake again!" said Andy. "Poor Jake! We do seem to be getting him into trouble!"

Another cave opened off the tunnel. It was smaller and not so well furnished as the one above. In it Sandy and Jake were quarrelling. The boys stopped to peep in for a moment. "Why, Jake is the hairy-legged man!" whispered Tom. "See his hairy legs and enormous feet!"

There was a fine old fight going on in Jake's cave. Roaring, shouting and yelling, chasing round and dodging! The boys wished they could stop and watch, but it was a good chance to slip by unnoticed. They dodged quickly past the entrance.

And now the tunnel dipped very steeply indeed, and went downwards for a long way.

"Into the very depths of the earth," said Tom in a hollow voice that quite startled Andy.

The walls of the rocky tunnel suddenly

began to gleam in a weird way. "Phosphor-escence," said Andy. "That's why it's glowing. It's almost unearthly!"

"Let's go back," said Tom suddenly. "I don't like this. And I don't like that funny noise right over our heads, either!"

"No, Tom, we can't go back now after coming all this way," Andy said. "We'll come out somewhere soon. We must! If only this tunnel would go upwards again. It's gone down so deep."

They went on again, between the gleaming walls. There was enough room in the passage for three men to walk abreast and the roof was well above their heads. They carried on walking, feeling very tired of the long, dark way. Andy was puzzled. Smugglers' Rock was not a big island. They could have walked across it by now! Where were they going? He suddenly stopped and clutched Tom's arm. Tom jumped violently. "Don't do that!" he said. "What's up?"

"Tom, I know where we are, and I know what that noise is!" said Andy, in an excited voice.

"What?" said Tom, looking at him, startled.

"It's the sea!" said Andy.

"Above our heads?" said Tom, looking up as if he expected to see waves breaking over him. "What do you mean?"

"We're under the rocky floor of the sea!" said Andy, in a loud voice. "We're in an underground tunnel, right under the sea itself – and I bet it goes to the Cliff of Birds."

Tom gawped. He was so astonished that he couldn't say a word. He listened to the dull, muffled boom above him. Yes, it must be waves pounding away, far up above their heads. Tom hoped the floor of the sea was strong! It wasn't nice to think of all that water up there.

"That's why the tunnel sloped so steeply," said Andy. "It goes right under the sea. Now we know how the smugglers take their goods to the Cliff of Birds! They carry them under the sea itself!"

"Come on," said Tom in excitement. "Come on, quick!"

CHAPTER TWENTY

An Unexpected Find

The boys went eagerly along the tunnel. It was wide enough for two train tracks. No wonder the smugglers could carry goods to the Cliff of Birds so easily! All the time the sea went on pounding away overhead.

"I hope," said Tom, "there isn't a leak in the roof! It would be awful if the sea began pouring in."

"Don't be silly! This tunnel must have existed for years," said Andy. "There's no reason why it should suddenly spring a leak! We're all right."

"I suppose we are," said Tom. "Oh! My torch is running out!"

"Well, we'll make do with just mine now," said Andy. "But we still have Zoe's torch if mine runs out. Walk close to me."

"I wonder who first found this passage," said Tom, stumbling over an uneven piece. "Hey, shine your torch more downwards,

Andy. I can't see where I'm going."

They went on for a long while. Surely they must be nearing the end of it now?

"Listen, that booming noise isn't nearly so loud," said Tom, suddenly stopping.

"You're right," said Andy. "That must mean we're out from under the sea and maybe under the Cliff of Birds."

"You know, Andy, I think we shall probably come up into that cave where I saw all those boxes and crates," said Tom. "When I was there, I saw Jake and the fisherman disappear down a hole in the floor of the cave, and I bet that hole led down into this tunnel."

"You're probably right," said Andy. "Come on, we'll soon see."

On they went again. The passage grew even wider as they stumbled forward. Then Andy's torch flashed on piles of cases in what looked like a big underground hall. Andy went over to them curiously.

"Each case has got some sort of scribbled letter or numbers on," he said. "Look at all those green ones, too."

"Here's one with the lid half broken," said Tom. "Bring the torch over. We might

be able to see what's inside."

The boys pulled out handfuls of straw, packing and padding material. Then Andy gave a long low whistle, and stood staring in astonishment. Tom looked at him impatiently. "What is it? Do you know what's inside?"

"Yes, look, see that shining barrel? There are guns in here. And ammunition in those green boxes over there! My word, this is more than smuggling."

"What is it then?" said Tom in a whisper. "I don't understand."

"Nor do I, yet," said Andy. "I only know that those men are bringing in thousands of guns, and ammunition, and sending them from here to somewhere else. No wonder those men sank our boat, kept us prisoner, and did all they could to prevent my father from finding us!"

Tom felt scared. "They won't hurt the girls, will they?" he said, thinking of Zoe and Pippa left alone in the cave.

"I don't think so," said Andy. "What are we to do? Somehow we must report this strange find, and we must get back to Zoe and Pippa! But how are we to do either?"

Tom sat down on a box. Things were happening too fast. He looked fearfully round the great underground storehouse. Guns! Guns by the thousand! Ammunition waiting to be used in harmful ways by evil people. He shivered.

Andy sat down beside him to think. The fisher boy looked very worried. He didn't know what the best thing to do was, and even if he did, how could he do it?

"The thing is," he said out loud, "should we try and get out of the tunnel on Smugglers' Rock, and find the girls, or should we go on and make our way into the Cliff of Birds? Perhaps that would be best, because we could go up the tunnel that leads to the waterfall, climb out of the opening, and wait to see if my father comes hunting for us again."

"Yes, that's a good idea," said Tom. "The men won't guess we have found the undersea tunnel and come to the Cliff of Birds. We could wait for our chance and signal from there."

"It sounds all right," said Andy rather gloomily, "but I doubt if my father will come again today. He's been two days running and found nothing. Maybe they're searching other places now."

"Still, it really is the only thing we can do," said Tom, getting up. "Come on, let's go."

They carried on cautiously. The tunnel narrowed after a while and became more as it had been before; a wide, rocky passage with a high roof. It ran upwards suddenly.

"I bet it's leading to that cave," whispered Tom. "Don't make a row, and shade your torch with your hand, Andy."

Moving very quietly now, the boys went on. The passage suddenly came to an abrupt end. A rocky wall barred their way!

"A dead end!" said Andy, feeling up and down it with his hands. "Oh no! What does this mean?"

It didn't seem to mean anything except that the passage had ended. They could go no further. Andy gave a huge sigh. He was exhausted from the long walk, and this was the last straw. He sat down suddenly, and Tom fell beside him, his legs shaking with tiredness.

"It's no good," said Andy. "I can't go back. I'm tired out!"

Tom felt the same. But after a short rest Andy felt more cheerful. He flashed his torch round again, and then suddenly turned it upwards, shining it above his head. He gave a cry and clutched Tom's arm.

"Look, what idiots we are! The way out is above our heads!"

Tom gazed up and saw a big round hole

in the roof. He gave a gasp. "Of course! Didn't I tell you those two men disappeared down a hole in the floor of their cave? Well, that's the hole, I bet! Why didn't we flash our torch upwards before?"

Both boys immediately felt better and leaped up, prepared to go on for miles again, if need be! Andy tried to see how to climb up, but couldn't find a way.

"What's that?" whispered Tom suddenly.

Andy shone his torch. He saw a rope caught round an iron staple driven into the rock. The rope was as dark as the rock, and neither of them had noticed it before.

"That's it, that's the way up and down!" whispered Andy. "We'll go up right away! I don't imagine there's anybody in the cave above, or we should see a light. I'll go first, you hold the torch."

Tom took the torch with trembling hands. Andy untwisted the rope and went up it like a monkey. He was used to ropes! Once he had climbed out of the hole, he found himself in darkness. He looked down and saw Tom's anxious face in the torchlight.

"Throw up the torch!" he said. "That's

it. Now, I'll shine it down for you. Catch hold of the rope. Come on!"

Tom climbed the rope and Andy gave him a helping hand at the top. They stood up and shone the torch round.

"Yes, this is the cave I told you about, the one with the stores," said Tom. "Good thing there's no one here!"

Andy examined the piles of boxes. "Those are food stores," he said. "See? That box is full of tinned food to feed all the men who help in this illegal work. Wow, someone planned this very thoroughly!"

"I'll show you where the underground river flows," said Tom, and dragged him behind the pile of boxes at one side of the cave. "That's where I jumped in!"

"Well, we won't go that way," said Andy. "It's too dangerous for my liking! We'll go up that twisting tunnel that leads to the waterfall opening, and we'll hope the torrent of water will be small enough today for us to creep out."

"And then we'll wait on the cliff and signal!" said Tom. "We'll soon be rescued!"

CHAPTER TWENTY-ONE

ANDY GETS A REAL SURPRISE

Tom was sure he knew the way. There was no chance of making a mistake, anyway, because as far as he remembered, once he had climbed up the steps out of the second cave, there had only been the one tunnel to follow. So, flashing their torches in front of them, the boys began the tiring journey upwards. It seemed longer to Tom than it had before.

"It's because it goes *up* this time, not down!" said Andy, who was panting too. "My, what a climb!"

After a time, Tom stopped in surprise. He shone his torch in front of him and stared, puzzled. "Look, Andy, the passage splits into two here! I felt sure there was only one way to follow. I can't have noticed it when I came down."

Andy examined the fork of the tunnel. "No, you wouldn't," he said. "You'd come round that dark corner and wouldn't see there was another way because of that jutting-out rock. Come on."

"But Andy, wait, I'm not sure which passage I came down!" said Tom. "I might have come by either."

"Well, it doesn't really matter," said Andy. "We'll take the right-hand one and hope for the best. If it doesn't lead out on the cliff, we can easily go back and take the other one."

"Yes, we could," said Tom, relieved. "Come on, then, let's take this one. I have a feeling it's the right one."

But he was wrong. The passage twisted and turned much more, and soon Tom was quite certain they were wrong.

"We'd better go back," he said.

"Well, I wonder where it leads to," said Andy, puzzled. "It must come to an end soon. We might as well just see what happens!"

So they went on, and were soon rewarded by sight of daylight shining far ahead. The passage suddenly came out from a deep cleft in the high cliff, and there, below them, was the sea. The boys sniffed the fresh air and felt the cool breeze on their faces. After the mustiness of the tunnel it was delicious. They sat down on the ledge.

"Now if we just had something to eat," said Tom. He put his hand into his pocket, and to his delight he found a piece of ham and half a piece of cake. The boys shared them hungrily, wishing there was more.

"We're higher up than we were before on the waterfall ledge," said Andy. "Let's lean over and see where we are exactly. We're not right at the top of the cliff. I think we've gone beyond the Cliff of Birds, and are now on a ledge the other side."

"You look down," said Tom. "I'll feel giddy!"

"Hold my legs then," said Andy. He lay flat on his tummy and worked himself to the edge of the ledge. Tom held his legs firmly.

Andy looked down. His eyes swept the coastline. It was as he had thought, they were no longer above the cove where they had anchored the *Andy*. They must be further round the coast. He examined the shore below closely and then he saw

something that made him stare so hard that his eyes blurred and he couldn't see.

"Hold me fast, Tom," he cried. "I'm going to wriggle a bit further forward, I must see what's exactly below us. Hold me tight!"

Tom tightened his grip on Andy's sturdy legs, as the boy hung himself a bit further over the ledge. He stared in silence for so long that Tom got impatient.

"What is it?" he said. "What can you see?"

Andy couldn't believe what he saw. He shut his eyes, and then opened them again. Yes, it was still there. How extraordinary, how very, very extraordinary! He slid back and sat up, his face glowing. His eyes shone so brightly that Tom was startled.

"Andy, what's up?" he said.

"Tom! Do you know what's down there, hidden in a little channel of water, in a fold of the cliff itself?" said Andy, in a voice that shook with excitement. "You'll never guess, never!"

"What?" cried Tom.

"Our boat!" yelled Andy, and beat on the rocky ledge with his hands. "The *Andy*!"

"But she's sunk," said Tom. "You know she is."

"I know she *isn't!*" said Andy. "Wouldn't I know my own boat? Those men were telling us lies. They haven't sunk the *Andy*! They've got her hidden in a very, very clever hiding place indeed!"

"But, Andy, oh, Andy, it can't be!" said Tom, a ridiculous tear spurting out from the corner of one eye. "I was sure she was sunk! How fortunate we took the wrong passage and got up here! We wouldn't have known about her if we hadn't, would we? What luck!"

"She hasn't been sunk!" said Andy joyfully. "We know where she's hidden. Now we've only got to get her, and we can sail home!"

"Yes, but how are we going to get her?" said Tom.

The two boys leaned against the rock and discussed what they should do now. Plainly they must try to get to the *Andy*. Then the difficult problem of escape would be solved.

"We can't possibly climb down the cliff here," said Andy. "It seems to me that the only thing to do is to get down to our own cove and climb round the rocks at the base of the cliff. It'll take ages!"

"Oh no, and we've got no food," said Tom dolefully. "That doesn't seem a very good idea to me."

"Well, think of a better idea then," said Andy. But of course Tom could think of nothing else at all.

"You're right," he said at last with a sigh. "It's the only thing to do. But let's get back to that store cave, where the boxes of food are kept, and have something to eat."

"All right," said Andy. "Anyway, I think it would be better to keep in hiding till the evening, in case anyone sees us clambering about the rocks. Come on, we'll get some food from the store cave, then take it up to the ledge by the waterfall and wait there till we think it's safe to climb down."

It was easier to get down to the store cave than it had been to climb from it up to the cliff! There was no one there. The boys hunted about and found some tin-openers and chose a few tins.

"Corned beef," said Tom, "and ham. And pears and apricots and plums. That's my selection!" They found some old bags to put them in. Each boy put some tins into a bag, threw it over his shoulder, and set out again to the cliff, but this time they took the other tunnel, when they came to the fork. Andy was amazed to see the caves where the torrent of water ran through, on its way to the waterfall.

"There's hardly any water pouring out today, luckily!" said Tom. "Come on, Andy, it'll be difficult wriggling along that narrow ledge to the entrance with our tins."

It was, but they managed it. And there they were at last, out on the ledge of the Cliff of Birds, and sitting down at the back of the shallow cave where Tom had left his ill-fated camera!

"Now for a meal!" said the very-hungry Tom. "And after that, all set to find the good old *Andy*!"

CHAPTER TWENTY-TWO

DOWN TO THE *ANDY* –
AND WHAT HAPPENED THERE

The boys had a good meal up on the ledge. They talked about the girls and wondered how they were getting on, and if they were all right.

"At any rate, they've got food," said Tom.

"Hey, what shall we do first when we get the *Andy*?" said Andy. "Go and rescue the girls, or run for home and report what we know?"

"I don't see how we can rescue the girls," said Tom. "We would only be seen by the men looking out for your father's boat, and they'd capture us again. We'd better run for home."

"Yes. I feel worried about the girls, though," said Andy, lying down on his back, unable to eat any more. "I'm afraid those men will be angry when they find we've escaped, and they'll make things unpleasant for Zoe and Pippa."

Andy fell asleep before he had time to worry any more about it. Tom drank the last drop of sweet juice from his tin, then lay back in the sunshine too, and shut his eyes. Both boys were exhausted from their exertions. They did not wake until the sun was well down. Andy sat up and shook Tom.

"Tom! Wake up! It's time we started to search for the *Andy*. The tide is going out, so the rocks will be fairly well uncovered."

Tom yawned as he sat up. He felt stiff. He did not like the thought of the long climb downwards. But it had to be faced. Andy went first, and Tom followed. When they were at the foot of the cliff, Andy turned westwards and began to clamber over the rocks. They were slippery with seaweed, but both boys were sure-footed and hardly slipped at all.

They made their way round the point and came in sight of another stretch of wild, rocky coast. Somewhere hidden along there was the *Andy*! But where? There was no sign of her from where they stood.

"Look, that's the way they brought her in," said Andy, pointing to a narrow sea path which was free of rocks.

Slowly they made their way along the rocks that skirted the cliff, looking for some bend that would mean the fold that hid the *Andy*. Then they rounded a steep rock, as tall as a church, and saw a deep-blue channel of water running into a fold of the cliff.

"This is it!" said Andy in delight. "See? Quite hidden except from above or here where we stand looking right in."

They went up the channel of water that lay in a hollowed-out piece of rock. There, at the end of it, lying quietly at anchor, was the *Andy*! The boys stood and stared at her in proud delight.

"Not sunk after all!" said Tom. "Poor old Andy, you were so miserable about that, weren't you?"

"Yes, more than I have ever been," said Andy. "Anyway, there she is. Is anyone about, do you think?"

Not a sound was to be heard except the usual wind and sea and bird noises. No one whistled, no one shouted. It seemed safe to go and explore the *Andy*. She hadn't got her sail up, but it was there on the deck. Andy saw that the oars had been put back too. Good!

The boys were soon on board. Andy examined her lovingly from top to toe. Yes, she was all right. No harm had come to her at all.

It was getting rather dark. Andy looked up at the sky. "I think we should set off now," he said. "It will be dark long before we get home, but we must chance the journey and hope we don't strike a rock. I know the way pretty well now."

The boys decided to row the *Andy* carefully out of the narrow little creek, and put up the sail as soon as they got out to sea. They were just about to haul up the anchor when Andy's sharp ears caught an unusual sound. He put his hand on Tom's arm. "Listen," he said. "Can you hear anything?"

Tom listened, trying to make out something besides the wind and the sea. At first he could hear nothing. Then he did hear something.

"Yes. I can hear the sound of some regular noise," he said, "a chug, chug, chug. Is it one of their motor-boats?"

"Yes, that's just it!" said Andy. "Oh, I hope it's not coming in here! Just as we were leaving too. The noise is getting louder, Tom, we'd better hide!"

The boys looked about for a hiding place.

"There's a good rock just over there," said Andy, pointing. "See where I mean? We can hide behind it and see everything. Hear everything too! Come on!"

The boys climbed quickly up to the big rock. They crouched down, waiting. Andy suddenly clutched Tom and pointed.

"There it is!" he whispered. "Look, coming along the little creek, up to the *Andy*. Pity it's so dark now. I can hardly see anything."

The motor-boat nosed its way up and came to rest beside the *Andy*. A man jumped out and called to someone else.

"It's Sandy," whispered Tom. "I think the other man is Jake. What are they going to do?"

A lamp was lit on the motor-boat, and another one was placed on the fishing boat nearby. Then Sandy and Jake got very busy. To and fro they went, carrying all kinds of

things. Andy suddenly recognised something and he gave a low exclamation that quite startled Tom.

"Look! That's our little cooking stove," whispered Andy. "You can just see it in the light of that lamp. They are putting it into the cabin of the *Andy*."

Then both boys were silent, for they were thinking the same thing. The stove had been in their snug cave on Smuggler's Rock. Were all the things from there being put back into the *Andy*? And if so, what was happening to the girls? The men must have climbed up to the cave, discovered that the boys were gone and then what had happened? Where could the girls be?

The boys were really worried. They couldn't bear to think of Zoe and Pippa in the hands of those grim smugglers. They were also puzzled why the men had brought the things back to the *Andy*. What was the sense of it? Why not leave them where they were?

The two men worked for some time, then they put out the light on the *Andy*, went back to the motor-boat, sat down and lit cigarettes.

"Are they going to stay here all night?" whispered Tom in dismay. "We'll never get away if they do!"

"Well, we can't leave till they go because they are blocking the way out," said Andy in a gloomy whisper. "Pity we didn't get off a few minutes sooner."

"They'd have seen us and given chase," said Tom. "It's just as well we didn't. But

I do wish they'd go. It would be so nice to get back home with the *Andy*, everything complete in her again!"

When they had smoked their cigarettes, the men got up. They had had very little to say to one another, and then only commonplace remarks. Andy wondered if Sandy was still angry with Jake for apparently stealing his food.

"We'll go and have a word with the Chief," said Sandy, throwing his glowing cigarette end into the water. "We'll see if anyone has found those dratted boys. Good thing we've got the girls to bargain with – nice little hostages they are!"

The men climbed on to a ledge, and made their way up the creek.

"Must be some entrance into the Cliff of Birds up that way," muttered Andy in Tom's ear. "I wonder who the Chief is? Perhaps that fellow with the glasses you once saw in the store cave with Sandy. I wonder how long they're going to be? I've a good mind to take their motor-boat and chance the run home in it! I know how to drive one!"

Tom was cold with evening wind, and

with suspense. He shivered now with excitement.

"What! Take their boat?" he said. "Would you really dare?"

CHAPTER TWENTY-THREE

WHO IS IN THE CABIN?

It was quite dark now. The sky was perfectly clear and the stars gave little light. Only the lamp on the motor-boat gleamed out, showing the deck.

Andy listened, but there was no sound of the men's voices. They had gone, but for how long? The boys had to act quickly. They got down from their hiding place and crept softly over the rocks to the motor-boat. They climbed over the sides, and examined it.

While they were looking to see how to start it up, they were startled by a noise in the cabin – a kind of long, drawn-out groan! The boys stood absolutely still, almost startled out of their wits, for they had been so certain they were alone. The groan came again.

"There's someone in that cabin!" whispered Andy in Tom's ear. "We'd better get out, quick! We don't want to be discovered here."

The boys made for their hiding place again, puzzled.

"Who's in there?" whispered Tom. "Who is it?"

"Goodness knows!" said Andy. "All I know is he's a frightful nuisance. Whoever he is, he has prevented us from taking the boat."

"What shall we do now?" whispered Tom. "We can't stay up here all night!"

"Those men will come back soon," said Andy. "Then maybe they'll push off and we can get going in the *Andy*. We'll have to wait and see."

"Can you hear any more groans?" asked Tom.

Andy shook his head. "No. They seem to have stopped."

A little later the noises began again. Then someone started hammering on the door. Someone shook the door violently and kicked it hard! The boys listened, more startled than ever.

Then they heard a voice they knew very well indeed, a voice muffled by the door of the cabin, but quite unmistakable! "Let me out! Where am I? You let me out or I'll kick the place down!"

The boys felt their hearts jump, and they stared down at the motor-boat in amazement.

"It's Zoe!" said Andy, forgetting to whisper in his great astonishment. "But what's Zoe doing there? Quick, let's go!"

The boys leaped down again, not caring whether or not they fell. Zoe was going mad with fury in the locked cabin. She was now hitting the door with something. Andy couldn't help smiling. He had seldom seen Zoe in a temper, but he knew she had one. He wondered if Pippa was there too. If so, she was very quiet.

Andy landed on the motor-boat first and ran to the cabin door. Zoe was now raining heavy blows on it, and shouting so loudly that she could not hear Andy's voice calling to her.

"Zoe! Zoe! Stop all that hammering so that I can unlock the door and get in! You'll hit me if you don't stop it!"

But the furious little girl went on and on, quite beside herself. *Crash, smash, crash!*

What in the world had she got in her hand?

There was a pause at last, and Zoe, plainly quite tired out, began to sob bitterly. Andy hammered on the door.

"Zoe! It's me, Andy! We're going to unlock the door and come in. Don't smash at it any more!"

There was silence inside the cabin. Zoe evidently couldn't believe her ears! Then there was a wild cry.

"Andy! Oh, Andy, unlock the door, quick!"

Andy unlocked and unbolted the door. Zoe flung herself on him and Tom, tears in her eyes.

"I thought you were lost for ever!" she sobbed. "We didn't know what to make of it when you didn't come back. The men said you never would. We thought you must be drowned!"

"Where's Pippa?" asked Tom.

"On that bunk in the cabin. She won't wake up," said Zoe. Andy took the lamp from the deck of the motor-boat and flashed the light on to where Pippa was lying.

"What's wrong with her?" he asked, hearing her breathing very loudly indeed.

"I don't know," said Zoe. "I think it must have been something those men gave us to drink. I didn't like the taste of mine, but Pippa drank all hers and then we fell fast asleep. I woke up just now and felt awfully sick, and I groaned and groaned."

"Yes, we heard you," said Andy. "You nearly broke that door down, Zoe! What did you hit it with?"

"That stool," said Zoe. "I felt so angry when I knew those men had put us somewhere and left us. I didn't know where we were, you see. We fell asleep in the cave high up in Smugglers' Rock."

"You've got a lot to tell us," said Andy. "And we've got some pretty peculiar things to tell you too. But it must wait because those men may come back at any time."

"No, this is our best chance to escape," said Tom. "But, Andy, we must tell them one thing!"

"Oh, yes!" said Andy. "Zoe, the *Andy* wasn't sunk! She's safe and sound – sails and oars and everything! Tom and I were just about to run home in her when Sandy and Jake brought this motor-boat up the creek and we had to hide."

"Oh, Andy!" said Zoe in joy. "I'm so glad. I was miserable about her, of course, but I knew you must be ten times more miserable!"

"We were almost at the top of the cliff when Andy saw her," said Tom. "He'd have fallen over with joy if I hadn't had hold of his ankles!"

Andy suddenly remembered that Sandy and Jake might come back at any moment. "Look here, we mustn't chatter like this," he said. "Tom and I were thinking of running for home in this motor-boat, as it is blocking our way and we can't get at the *Andy*."

"Well, let's go, then!" said Zoe eagerly. "It's really dark, though. I don't know how you'll see your way."

A groan from the cabin bunk made them jump. It was Pippa, waking up after her long sleep, feeling sick. Zoe went to her.

"It's all right, Pippa. You'll soon feel all right."

Pippa, still half asleep, groaned again. The two boys helped Pippa up on to the deck. The cool wind on her face was very refreshing. She soon stopped groaning.

"I feel a bit better," she said feebly. "Tom, Andy, why are you here? Where are we?"

"There's no time to tell you now," said Andy. "We must get going. Zoe and Tom can tell you everything on the way."

He went to start the engine of the motor-boat. But no matter how hard he tried, all it made was a humming noise. Andy could have cried!

"What's up?" said Tom. "Can't you get her going? Here, let me have a try!"

They all had a go, but nobody could

make the motor-boat start. It was most aggravating, especially as they couldn't leave on the *Andy* because the motor-boat was in the way!

"Look out, there's someone coming," said Tom, suddenly. "See the light of their cigarettes?"

"Skip out of the boat quickly!" whispered Andy. "Shut the cabin door, Tom, and lock it. The men may slip off without looking in and seeing that the girls aren't there. If they go, we can all get away in the *Andy*. Hurry!"

Tom locked and bolted the door of the cabin. Then he joined the others on the ledge and they all crept behind a rock. Sandy and Jake came along, talking. They clambered on board their boat.

The children hardly dared to breathe. Would the men be able to start up the engine and go? How they hoped that they would hear the roar of the engine and know that it would take the boat away. Then they could climb into the *Andy* and off they would go!

They heard Jake's voice. "Those girls all right, do you think, Sandy? They ought to have woken up by now. That sleeping draught you gave them wasn't too strong, was it?"

"Aw, let them alone," came Sandy's hoarse voice. "What does it matter if I gave it to them strong? Keep them quiet! We'll carry them over to their boat and lock them in the cabin. No one will ever know where they are. And if those two boys ever get back and split on us, well, we'll have those girls as hostages. Our safety against theirs!"

"Well, I'll get one of them now," said Jake, and he unlocked the cabin door. "Here, give me the lamp."

There was a moment's silence as he took the lamp and swung it into the cabin. Then he gave a loud cry.

"What's this? There's nobody here! Those two girls have gone!"

CHAPTER TWENTY-FOUR

ANDY HAS A GOOD IDEA

Sandy and Jake were amazed to find their two prisoners gone. The children heard their astonished remarks as they searched the little cabin.

"But the door was still locked and bolted! How could they have gone?"

"Kids can't walk through locked doors, and there's no window they could open."

"We left them fast asleep. I looked in at them before we went, and locked and bolted the door afterwards!"

"I know. I saw you."

"Then what's happened to them? Here's the cabin, just as it was when we left it, locked and bolted, and we come back to find it still locked and bolted and the kids gone. I don't like it."

"Look here, do you suppose anyone came along and let them out, and locked and bolted the door again?" Sandy's hoarse voice said. There was a pause before Jake answered.

"It's possible, but who's about in the middle of the night in this lonely place? Nobody! It's very strange! Shall we go and tell the Chief?"

"Not me!" said Sandy at once. "What do you think he'd say to us if he knew his two precious prisoners were gone, his only means of bargaining if this little game gets reported! No, Jake, we've got to find those girls. They can't be far away, can they?"

"No. You're right," said Jake. "Their own fishing boat is still here, and they're not likely to swim down this creek or climb the cliff either, unless they want to break their necks."

"Search the motor-boat first," said Sandy. "And then the fishing boat over there. It's a pity we didn't carry them there, dump them down in the cabin and bolt the hatch over them."

"Well, if they could get out of a locked and bolted door here, they could have got out of a bolted cabin in their own boat," said Jake. "Come on, they're not on our boat. Let's look around these rocks."

The children began to tremble. Sandy and Jake were two fierce, angry men. It would not be pleasant to be found by them. Andy frowned. What could he do to distract them?

An idea came to him. He bent down and groped about for a piece of rock. He found one and stood up. He tried to make out where the *Andy* was, and then, taking aim, he flung the rock as hard as he could in her direction. It fell on the deck of the fishing boat with a loud crash that echoed up and down the little creek.

Tom, Zoe and Pippa jumped violently. They had not known what Andy was going to do. But Sandy and Jake jumped even more violently!

"Here! Did you hear that?" said Sandy's voice. "What was it? It sounded as if it came from the fishing boat. That's where they are! Come on, quick. We'll get them, the tiresome little brats!"

Forgetting all about searching the rocks, the two men hurried to where the *Andy* floated. They climbed on deck, and Andy climbed after them, as soft-footed as a cat. A wild plan was in his head. He didn't know

196

if he could carry it out or not, but it was worth trying!

The men flashed their torches about the boat.

"They'll be down in the cabin!" said Sandy. "Come on. Wait till I get hold of them!"

He opened the hatch and leaped down into the little cabin. Jake stood above it, looking down. And suddenly something happened to him that gave him the shock of his life! Something hurled itself at his back and made him lose his balance! He gave a shout of terror, and then fell headlong down the open hatch into the cabin below. He fell on top of the equally startled Sandy, who toppled over and struck his head hard against the wooden table.

His torch flew out of his hand, its light going out. The little cabin was in darkness. Sandy, quite sure that some unexpected enemy had fallen upon him to kill him, began to fight like a madman. He struck out unmercifully at the horrified Jake, who tried in vain to stop him and had to hammer back in self-defence! The two men rolled over and over, pummelling each other, yelling and shouting for all they were worth!

It was pitch-black in the cabin. Andy flashed his torch down and grinned with delight to see the rogues going for each other. Let them get on with it! He slammed down the hatch, and bolted it. The noise startled the two men and they stopped fighting. It also startled the three hidden children and they jumped.

"What was that?" whispered Zoe. "I wish I could see what's happening!"

A cheerful voice came through the darkness. "All right, everyone?"

"Yes, Andy! But what was all that noise?" called back Tom, glad to hear Andy's voice again.

"Oh, Sandy went down into the cabin, and I shoved Jake in to keep him company," said Andy, still more cheerfully. "I don't think Sandy welcomed Jake because they've been fighting like wild cats! The slam you heard was the hatch closing. It's well and truly bolted!"

"Andy! You've got them prisoner! Well done!"

Soon the four were on the fishing boat,

and Andy told them proudly once more how he had made the two men prisoners. It seemed too good to be true!

"Make as much noise as you like!" Andy yelled down to them gleefully. "You won't be able to get out."

"Are they really caught?" asked Pippa, sitting down on the deck. "Oh dear, all this has made me feel ill again!"

"You'll soon be all right, Pippa," said Zoe. "I feel quite better now. Wow, Andy, that was a good trick of yours! What are we going to do next?"

"Well, I don't think anyone will be along this way tonight, so we can let those two fellows shout all they want to!" said Andy. "When dawn comes we'll release the motor-boat, and somehow get her down the creek and out of the way of the *Andy*. Then we'll take the *Andy* and run for home."

"With Sandy and Jake?" asked Tom, his eyes wide with excitement.

"Well, they'll have to come too, whether they want to or not," said Andy with a grin. "Two prisoners who will have to explain a lot of things very soon."

"I'll be glad to get home safely," said

Zoe. "Mummy must be so worried."

"We'll all be glad to get home," said Andy. "I vote we rest till dawn. We can't mess about with the motor-boat while it's dark."

"Oh, Andy, we've slept for ages!" said Zoe. "Can't we talk? I want to swap stories about our adventures."

"Well, fire away," said Andy. "Tom and I have had a good sleep today too. Let's get back to the motor-boat and talk in the cabin there. Sandy and Jake have got all our rugs down in our cabin!"

The four went to the motor-boat and curled up in the bunks there. They lit the lamp and soon it looked quite cosy.

"Did anything much happen after we had gone?" asked Andy.

"Well, Pippa and I didn't hear you leave the cave when you went to follow the trail of shells," said Zoe. "We didn't wake up till morning. We remembered where you'd gone, of course, and hoped you wouldn't be too long. We had breakfast, and then we squeezed out of the cave to wait."

"You didn't come," said Pippa. "So we thought we would follow the trail of shells ourselves, and see if we could find you! We followed them and came to where they stopped . . ."

"I bet you didn't know where to go next!" interrupted Tom.

"We didn't," said Zoe. "We couldn't imagine why the shells ended at a blank wall of rock. And then suddenly the rock opened!"

"Wow!" said Tom. "That must have scared you!"

"It did," said Zoe. "We ran away, but that bandy-legged man tracked us back to our cave and yelled to us to come out."

"We had to come out in the end," said Pippa, "because he threatened to smoke us out again. He thought you boys were in there and he yelled and yelled for you to come out too. When you didn't, he crawled in and found the cave empty!"

"What did he do then?" asked Andy, with great interest.

"He tried to make us say where you were," said Pippa. "He was horrible. Then he hunted about all over the place and still couldn't find you. Then some other men came, and they had a sort of meeting. We couldn't hear what they said."

"They sent Sandy into our cave and he brought out everything," said Zoe. "Then we were taken, blindfolded as before, back to that high cave in Smugglers' Rock. We didn't have any food or drink for ages, and then Sandy came with some."

"And we think that what we drank must have had sleeping medicine in it," said Pippa, "because after we'd drunk it, we simply couldn't keep our eyes open!"

"Creeps!" said Andy. "They meant to bring you here and lock you in the *Andy*, keeping you as hostages in case Tom and I had escaped, and were going to report the whole affair to someone. What a bit of luck we happened to be here too!"

"Yes! Now tell us how you came to be here!" begged Zoe. "Go on, you must tell us everything."

So Andy and Tom told their tale too, and when they had finished, dawn was rising and it was time to get to work again. With luck they should be home that day and what a lot of news they had to bring!

CHAPTER TWENTY-FIVE

RUNNING FOR HOME

Daylight filtered into the narrow creek and gave the children just enough light to see by. The boys tried once more to start the engine of the motor-boat. But they could not get it going.

"Let's untie her and give her a jolly good push!" said Andy. "Perhaps she'll float away and give us room to get out."

So they untied the rope, and all together the children shoved. The boat slid away from the ledge they stood on and floated down the creek.

"She's going!" cried Zoe. "She's going to sea all by herself!"

"Now she's stuck," said Andy, as the boat wedged herself against a rock. "I'll climb on to the motor-boat and push her along with an oar."

Tom fetched him an oar from the *Andy*. Andy ran down the ledge, jumped to a rock, and from there to the deck of the motor-boat.

She bobbed there, not seeming to know which way to go. Andy shoved again.

"There she goes, down the creek," yelled Tom. "Oh, come on out, Andy, or you'll go with her!"

But Andy did not get out of the motor-boat till she was right out of the channel. Then he clambered over the side, slithered down to a rock, and began to wade back to the rocky ledge that ran beside the creek.

He went back to the others, grinning. "Well, the motor-boat's out of our way all right!" he said. "Now to get the *Andy* out. We'll have to use the oars. We'll put up the sail when we get the wind."

Sandy and Jake began making a great noise again down in the cabin of the *Andy*. They knew that something was up! But no matter how hard they tried they couldn't make the bolted hatch budge.

"Make all the noise you like!" Andy called to the men cheerfully. "We don't mind! By the way, your motor-boat's been turned loose. I hope it won't smash to pieces on the rocks!"

The children laughed as the terrible threats came up from the cabin. They were feeling very happy. They had the *Andy* back, they were all together again, they had two prisoners and a wonderful secret.

They had a quick meal from the tins that Tom and Andy had brought down from the cave and then they set off. The children worked away with the oars, getting the *Andy* carefully down the little creek until at last it was bobbing on the open sea. The tide was running very high indeed.

"Tom, take the oars and keep her off those rocks," said Andy. "I'll hoist the sail. Zoe, take the tiller. Keep her headed the way she is."

Andy was just about to put up the sail, when he heard a cry from Pippa. "Oh look, the motor-boat is going on the rocks! Look at her!"

The children looked. Pippa was right. The motor-boat was indeed on the rocks! With no one to control her she was quite at the mercy of the waves. There was a smashing, grinding noise. The children's faces grew solemn.

"Don't let's watch any more," said Tom.

"It's awful to see the waves smashing it up. It's on its side now and look at that great hole! When it's next swept off the rocks, it will fill with water and sink."

"One less boat for the smugglers," said Andy, and put up the sail.

The sail filled with wind and flapped eagerly. Andy slid down to the seat by the tiller and took it from Zoe. "Bring in the oars, Tom," he said. "We're all right now. Off we go with the wind!"

It was glorious to feel the little boat leaping along. "If she could sing, she would!" said Pippa.

There came a noise from below. The children listened, trying to make out the voice against the sound of wind and waves.

"It's only Sandy saying that they feel sick down there and want some fresh air," said Tom, with a grin.

Zoe put her mouth to the crack of the hatch and called down. "You made me and Pippa feel sick with your horrible drug. It's your turn now! You won't come up here!"

"Definitely not!" said Andy, and swung the tiller round.

Plainly Sandy and Jake didn't feel there

was much hope for it, for they said no more. The children forgot about them as they raced along. They revelled in the speed of their boat, and loved the way she seemed to gallop over the white-topped waves.

"Good old Andy!" thought Zoe, looking at him. "He's got back his boat, and he's happy again!"

The boat swept over the waves, and they made very good time indeed. "We'll be home about eleven, at this rate!" shouted Andy.

They entered their home waters just after eleven, the red sail making a bright speck on the blue waters. The children wondered if their mother and Andy's father would be there. It was unlikely, because they didn't know the children were coming home!

But they were there! Someone had sighted the *Andy* as she turned into the harbour and the word was sent round at once.

"The *Andy* is back! There she is! Let's hope the children are safe and sound!"

The children's mother was fetched and she ran down to the jetty, her face bright with hope. She'd been very worried. Andy's father stood there too, watching the incoming boat. Then a shout went up.

"They're all on board, all four of them. They're safe!"

Andy's father turned to the children's mother. "They're safe, ma'am," he said, his eyes shining. "I knew they'd be all right with my Andy. Look at them waving to us!"

The *Andy* stopped beside the jetty, and while helping hands made it safe, the children leaped off and ran to their mother. Andy got a big hug from his father, and then he pointed back to the boat.

"We've two prisoners bolted down in the cabin, Dad. Look out for them, they're pretty dangerous fellows."

Everyone gaped. Andy's father rapped out a few questions and Andy answered breathlessly. Having heard, three stalwart, sturdy fishermen started grimly towards the *Andy*. They opened the hatch, and up came Sandy and Jake, looking very green. They were grasped by rough, strong hands and jerked off the deck to the jetty.

"It's a case for the police, Dad," said Andy. "There's something very strange

going on at the Cliff of Birds and
Smugglers' Rock. We found dozens of cases
of guns and ammunition."

The fishermen whistled and looked at
one another. One of them went off to fetch
the local policeman. It was all very exciting
indeed!

"I'm hungry," said Tom. The girls laughed. It was so like Tom to say that, in the middle of all the excitement. His mother put her arm round them.

"Come along and have a good meal," she said. "I'm so happy to have you back. You've no idea how worried I've been. Andy's father and uncle, and many of the other fishermen, all went out looking for you, but there wasn't a trace to be found! I'm longing to hear every single thing."

Andy and his father went with them. Sandy and Jake were left with the fishermen until the policeman came. Tom wondered what his mother had got to eat.

While Andy and the others were sitting down to a noisy and exciting meal, many things were happening. The policeman decided that all these curious affairs that the children had reported were quite beyond him, and he had rung up the superintendent in the next big town.

The superintendent, listening carefully, had been filled with amazement. Yes, certainly this was a very big affair indeed. He telephoned to headquarters and soon dozens of telephone lines were humming with news and instructions.

Sandy and Jake were safely in prison and, fearful of their own skins, they gave away all the secrets of their Chief. The children knew nothing of this, but laughed and chattered as they told their mother all that had happened. They had quite forgotten how frightened they had been.

"When things end well, nothing seems to matter," said Tom. "I wonder what will happen to those smugglers!"

CHAPTER TWENTY-SIX

THE END OF IT ALL

That evening, when the children really thought they had nothing more to say, a very large shiny car drove up to the cottage. A neat, well-dressed little man with sharp, clever eyes stepped out.

"You don't know who I am," he said, "but I am in charge of certain affairs and I want to ask you a few questions. My name is Colonel Rupert Knox. I've heard most of your story from Andy's father. Now, can you tell me this: did you ever see the man that Sandy and Jake call the Chief?"

"Well, I did see a man once in the store cave with Jake, a man wearing glasses, but dressed like a fisherman," said Tom. "I don't know if he was the Chief though."

"No. That wasn't the Chief," said the sharp-eyed man. "Jake has told us who that man was. We are hoping to get him tomorrow, with all the others."

"What are you going to do?" asked Tom with great interest.

"We're going to round up all the smugglers and their boats," said Colonel Knox. "We're combing the passages and tunnels and caves. We're opening every case and box and crate. We shall cross-examine every man we get, and we shall set that great lamp burning and watch for the ships that answer the signal. We shall get them too!"

"Why did they smuggle those guns and things in?" said Zoe.

"There is a country that is not allowed to import firearms," said the Colonel. "The ones you found were made in a distant land, and have been smuggled here to take across to this country. As you can imagine, very high prices are paid. Men in our country have been acting as a go-between, that is, they smuggle the arms here, and, for a price, take them to the buyers. They make a fortune out of it."

"Oh," said the children, wide-eyed and astonished. Andy considered a moment.

"And the man you'd really like to get hold of is the one they call the Chief?" he said. Colonel Knox nodded.

"Yes. All the other fellows merely obey orders. He's the big brain behind it all. We've suspected something for a long time, but we couldn't find out how the firearms were brought here, or where, nor did we know who was behind it."

"And if you don't get him, he'll probably start off again somewhere else?" said Tom. "Well, I wish we could tell you who he is. Don't Sandy and Jake know?"

"No, all they know is that he is a tall fellow, who always wears a mask when visiting them," said Colonel Knox. "And they think he lives in the nearest big town, so that he can get to the Cliff of Birds in a short time, when he needs to. But as there are about fifty thousand people living in that town, it's like looking for a needle in a haystack!"

"I see," said Andy. "I do hope you get him, Colonel Knox. Wasn't it a bit of luck we stumbled on their haunt? It was quite an accident."

"A very happy accident for us!" said the Colonel. "We don't want our country mixed up in affairs of this sort."

"I wonder how the Chief gets the goods out of the Cliff of Birds and Smugglers' Rock," said Andy, puzzled.

"We're not quite sure yet," said Colonel Knox. "But we think there is another way out of the Cliff of Birds, leading to a flat piece of ground at the back, a good place for aeroplanes to land. It is likely that the Chief took off loads of firearms in his planes."

"My word!" said Tom. "What a dangerous plot we found! I wonder the men didn't guard us more carefully!"

"They didn't know what wily birds you were!" said the Colonel, with a laugh. "But they meant to use the two girls as hostages, if you got home and reported their doings. That would have been very unpleasant for Zoe and Pippa, and I'm afraid we would have had to let the miscreants free rather than risk anything happening to the girls."

"It's a good thing we captured Sandy and Jake then," said Andy.

"A very good thing," said Colonel Knox. "They gave us a tremendous amount of valuable information. It's just the Chief we can't seem to lay our hands on."

"It's a pity we never saw him," said Tom.

"A great pity," agreed Colonel Knox. "Well, I'm proud to have met you, you're a brave, adventurous four! I must go now, but I want you to come over to the big town where I live and have lunch with me tomorrow. Will you do that?"

"Oh, yes!" cried the four.

"But how can we get there?" asked Zoe. "There's only one train."

"I'll send my car for you," said Colonel Knox, and got up to go. The children took him to his sleek black car.

"He's clever and kind and goes straight to the point in everything," said Tom. "I only wish we could tell him who the Chief of the smugglers is."

The next day the car was sent to fetch the four children. It whisked them away to the grandest hotel in the town, where Colonel Knox met them at the door. They felt most important walking in with him and when Tom read the menu he looked at his host in awe.

"Can we have all these things?" he said. "Oh, it will be the best meal we've ever had. Look, it says 'Mixed ice creams' at the bottom. Can we have vanilla, strawberry and chocolate all together?"

"Yes, and coffee ice cream as well, I believe," said Colonel Knox, laughing. "Well, sit down. Now, what would you like to drink?"

Soon the children were in the middle of a most glorious meal. Tom looked blissfully happy. This was a wonderful reward for all the adventures they had been through. He was in the middle of his ice cream when he looked up and saw a man seating himself at a nearby table. He was a tall, burly fellow, with deep-set eyes and black wavy hair.

"Who's that?" asked Tom in a low voice. The Colonel looked surprised.

"Oh, just someone who lives in this town," he said. "One of the very richest, though you wouldn't think it to look at him."

Tom stared at the man curiously. He certainly didn't look rich, for the sleeve of his coat wanted mending. His red shirt was open at the neck, and lacked a button halfway down.

Tom suddenly went as red as a beetroot with excitement. He began burrowing in his pockets.

"What's wrong with you?" said Andy.

Tom brought something out from his pocket. He pushed it across to Colonel Knox, who looked at it in surprise, thinking that Tom had suddenly gone mad.

"Sir," said Tom in a whisper. "I found that red pearl button in a cave in the Cliff of Birds. It must have belonged to one of the men there, though I never saw one with a red shirt on. But look at that man over there. He's got on a red shirt, and it has buttons exactly like this, and one is missing!"

Colonel Knox's eyes flashed from Tom's button to the man's shirt. He slipped the button into his pocket.

"Say no more now," he commanded. "Don't even look at the fellow. Do you understand?"

There was something in those commanding tones that made the children feel a little frightened. Colonel Knox scribbled a note, beckoned to a waiter and told him to deliver it somewhere. Then the Colonel became his own charming, joking self again.

"I'll let you know if your button has solved our problem," he said to Tom, when the man got up and went. "It may have! It may have! He's the one man we never even suspected. Good for you, Tom! My word, this is a great affair, and no mistake!"

So it was! Before long all the motor-boats in the cove had been taken, the crews too, and every smuggler found in the caves. The smuggled goods had been confiscated, ships that helped in the smuggling were captured, and the whole plot exposed.

And the man in the red shirt was the leader, the Chief of the whole gang! It was highly fortunate that Tom should have found the button that led to his capture. Colonel Knox was very pleased indeed.

"You shall have a new camera for your help!" he said to Tom. "Without you we should never have known who the Chief was. No one even suspected him! He ran the whole business very cleverly indeed, and not even the men themselves ever saw him face to face. He has made a fortune, but he won't make any money for many years to come!"

"What a lot has happened in a week or so!" said Zoe, as they all sat on the jetty that night, waiting for the fishing boat to come back with Andy and his father. "Look, there she goes! Leading all the rest of the boats as usual. Ahoy, Andy, ahoy! We're waiting for you!"

Their mother came up to see the fishing boats sail in. As Andy stepped on to the jetty, Tom turned eagerly to his mother.

"Mum! Can we go out with Andy in his boat next week, when he has a day off? I know a lovely place I'd like to go to."

"Certainly not!" said his mother. "What, lose you again for days on end, and not know where you are? My dears, I shall never, ever let you go out alone with Andy again! I just don't know what might happen next!"